AGE OF END:
KINGS AND CROWNS

AGE OF END: KINGS AND CROWNS
by Chris Yee

Copyright © 2016 by Chris Yee. All rights reserved.

This is a work of fiction. Any resemblance to actual persons living or dead, businesses, events or locales is purely coincidental. Reproduction in whole or part of this publication without express written consent is strictly prohibited.

ISBN 978-0-9973536-3-1

Cover designed by Rebecca Frank
http://RebeccaFrank.design

Published by To The Moon Publishing
www.tothemoonpublish.com

ONE

THERE WAS A room, walls lined with monitors. Screens on top of screens, side by side, emitting an aura of video footage. In the center of the room, sitting on a rolling chair, was Charlotte.

Her eyes were glued to the wall of monitors. She watched in amazement as Vince and the others sailed across the ocean. She was fascinated by the events in the cave. She knew Barnabus was a loose cannon, but slaughtering everyone in the cage? Greene would not be pleased. And now Vince and Saul were on their way. She scribbled notes into her journal, keeping track of everything.

A man popped his head in the room. "It's happening again. More bombings."

"More?" she said. "Christ, Trevor. Sometimes I just don't know about this world. Do you think we're safe?"

"Oh yeah. There's no way they're getting through the walls. Anything interesting happen in here?"

Charlotte leaned back in her chair. "You have no idea. Barnabus is dead. Vince shot him with his own gun."

"I can't say I'm surprised. It was bound to happen at some point. The man got stabbed in the eye on his first assignment. He was careless. Always has been."

"He had it coming, too. That crazy son of a bitch slaughtered all of Greene's subjects. Dismembered them in the cage."

"Holy crap! I've talked to him a few times. He did seem a little off his rocker."

"I know, right? He gave me the creeps."

"But your name sounds so similar to his."

"Ugh, don't remind me. Marble was such a pleasant last name, until I met Barnabus Carbul, weirdo of the century. I don't know why Greene likes him so much."

"They go way back. They've been working together for a long time. He's about as loyal as they get."

"Until he snaps and goes on a murdering spree."

Trevor chuckled. "Yeah, well, not everyone's perfect."

Charlotte glanced back at the wall of screens. "Anyway, now Vince, Saul, and the others are headed this way. They took his boat and their sailing across the ocean right now. They say they're going to stop Greene. Saul's pretty injured, too. Barnabus shot him. I think he's going to die."

"Wow. You've seen some exciting stuff these last few days."

"Jealous?"

He smiled. "Cosmetic test subjects aren't nearly as exciting. You really lucked out getting assigned to the vitality sector."

"Luck had nothing to do with it. I worked hard to get where I am."

"I know. I'm just teasing you."

A rumble came from outside. Charlotte turned. "Are you sure we're safe? Those bombs sound close."

"There are three walls around the Spire, all armed with cannons. We'll be fine. That's probably just our guys firing back."

The lights in the room turned red, and the alarm blared over the speakers. A loud automated voice called out. "Potential spire breach. Secure all data and proceed to your designated safe room."

Charlotte took one last look at the screens against the wall, hit the record button, and grabbed her journal. "So much for safe. Think we'll finally get to use the evacuation pods?" She walked through the door.

Trevor followed as they walked down the hall. "The alarm sounds if they breach the first wall. They've still got two more to go. There's no way that will happen. It never has before."

"You never know. Simon is resourceful."

"Simon is a crazy terrorist with a messed up sense of justice. He plays dirty."

"Even more reason to take this seriously."

Trevor shrugged. "I am taking it seriously. I'm just confident in Greene's security."

"You shouldn't be overconfident. It leads to embarrassment."

"There's nothing wrong with being confident."

"There is if it gets you killed. That's how Saul got shot. He didn't think Barnabus would do it. But when it comes to people like Barnabus, or Simon, you always proceed with caution. There's no telling what they'll do. The crazy are unpredictable."

"Where does Greene fall on your crazy-scale?"

She looked around to see if anyone was listening, and then lowered her voice. "I don't believe in everything Greene stands for, but the man has principles, and he sticks to them. I respect that. Simon is just a savage."

They turned the corner and headed towards the safe room at the other end of the hallway. "You don't believe in what he stands for, huh? This is the first time I'm hearing this."

"Keep your voice down. It's not really something I want to advertise. I probably shouldn't have even mentioned it."

"You're right, you shouldn't have. That kind of talk will get you fired. Or thrown in prison."

"I wouldn't get thrown in prison."

"You would. Have you seen the cell room? Do you have any idea how many of those people committed treason?"

"But those are terrorists. Members of the Crowns. He wouldn't lock one of his workers up with them."

"Are you sure about that? I've never met the man, but I hear he can hold a grudge."

"Just don't mention this to anyone else and I won't have to worry."

"My lips are sealed."

They reached the end of the hall and entered the safe room. Everyone else was already there. "Took you long enough," said the man in front. "We've been waiting. You know there are terrorists out there, right? You could have picked it up a little."

Charlotte sighed. "Calm down. They won't even make it past the second wall." She pressed the red button and the door locked behind her.

TWO

ELLA STARED STRAIGHT ahead. She watched the waves rise and fall. She turned to see where she was. She stood in the middle of a raft, all alone. A vast ocean, and nothing else. Why was she here? She spun around to examine her surroundings. Up in the sky, a seagull flew over her head. Her eyes followed the bird as it dove down and crashed into the water.

A thunderous bang came from behind. She turned around to find herself in a prison cell. She grabbed the metal bars and tried to scream, but nothing came out. Her voice did not work. Water dripped in the corner of her cell. She struck the bars with her boot. No sound. The whole world was muted. Just the dripping of water on cobblestone. She stared at the corner, watching each drop hit the ground.

"He will see you now."

The voice startled her. She whipped around, but no one was there. The cell door was now open. She wandered out and down the dark hallway. Further down, she could see a light. She walked towards it.

The path ended and opened up to a large courtyard. Colorful flowers filled the place with bright yellows and pinks. In the middle of the courtyard was a figure cloaked in green. In front of him stood familiar faces. Rupert. Alan. Vince. Saul. They all stood facing Ella, blank looks on their faces. The green figure paced behind them. His face was hidden in shadow. He stopped behind Saul, placed his hand upon his head, and whispered, "Bang."

Saul's head exploded into a pulpy mess.

THREE

ELLA JUMPED AWAKE drenched in sweat. The blinding sun beat down on her skin.

"Are you okay, Ella?" Vince asked. He and Saul were still paddling.

"Bad dream." She looked around. The others were out cold. The wall looked much larger now that they were up close. It shot up thirty stories, maybe more. Poking up from behind it was a single large tower, coming to a pointy tip near the top.

Vince gazed up. "It's impressive, isn't it?"

"Yes, it is. How is it even possible? To build a wall this long, it would take ages." She turned left and right to see the wall stretch both ways. "It just keeps going. It doesn't end. How are we going to get in?"

"I don't know. We'll have to get closer to inspect it. Maybe there's a door or gate. We've been out here a while. When we saw that tower, we thought it was a good place to start."

An explosion rumbled from the other side of the wall. Shortly after, smoke rose up from behind.

"Something crazy is going on in there," Saul said. "Some sort of fight or something."

Another explosion went off. This one woke the others. Alan sprung up. "What was that?"

"The City," Ella said. "There's something going on in there."

Alan stared at the wall, awestruck. "I've never seen anything this big."

Rupert nodded. "It is quite amazing."

"And this is just a wall. Imagine what it's like inside."

Vince stopped paddling and turned around. "No matter how nice it is inside, you must all remember that these are dangerous people. We must not get distracted by their impressive technology. We are here for one reason. To stop them. To free whatever prisoners they have and put an end to their experiments."

"We hear you loud and clear," Alan said. "We stick to our mission. For Patrick."

They all repeated. "For Patrick."

Another explosion went off, further down the wall. Pieces of stone and debris crumbled from the top as a crack began to form. They watched the puff of smoke rise above the wall. A fourth explosion. This time, the crack split open and a chunk of the stone came hurtling into the water. A fifth. The crack shattered along the wall and down to the bottom. Large chunks flew off and the remainder of the stone crumbled down. In its place was a gaping hole.

"There's our entrance," Vince said.

Alan looked at the opening. "Are you sure we want to go *towards* the explosions?"

"It's our only way in."

"Let's wait for them to stop first before we go rushing in. It's not like the hole is going to close back up."

"No," Vince said. "We can use the situation to our advantage. Whatever is going on in there, it's creating chaos. Confusion. If we wait, we'll have to answer to someone. If we go now, we can sneak through unnoticed."

Saul nodded. "I'm with Vince. After killing one of their men and stealing their boat, the last thing we want is to get noticed. Especially if this Greene guy has his eye out for us. I say we go now while we still can."

The others nodded in agreement.

Saul pointed to the falcon on Rupert's shoulder. "Can he—"

"She," Rupert interrupted.

"Sorry. Can she fly ahead and scout the area?"

Rupert stroked the back of her neck. "I'm afraid not. She was injured back in the cave. Her wing is banged up."

"Then I guess we're going in blind. Still, this is our best chance."

Vince handed out the extra paddles. "Alright, let's go."

They paddled towards the opening. As they got closer, the explosions grew louder and more frequent. A mix of dust, dirt, and sand floated through the air and concealed their entry as they crossed over the City border. Screams came from every direction. Bombs went off everywhere.

Vince stepped from the raft to solid ground. As he helped the others, a man approached. His clothes were torn and his face was smudged with soot. He glanced at the raft. "Ha! Escaping, are ya?" he yelled. "Live free forever, brothers!" Then he tilted his head. "Wait a second. You're not getting *on* the raft. You're getting *off*. You're from the outside." As he said this, five other men strolled up behind him.

Vince watched them cautiously. "That's none of your business. Leave us be."

The man smiled. "It is my business. You see, outsiders are good bargaining chips. Greene has some of our men. Your group will make a fair trade."

Saul stepped forward. "What makes you think we'll come with you?" He stood tall and puffed out his chest, but winced from the pain in his stomach.

The man saw his bloodstained shirt and smiled even wider. His front tooth was crooked. "You're a little weak there, aren't you, buddy?" He pulled out a gun. The five men behind him did the same. "I have no doubt you folks will come with us."

FOUR

L ED BY CROOKED Tooth, the six men escorted them through the streets at gunpoint. Dust and smoke filled the air, obscuring their sight. Men and women, all in dull clothes, gripping bombs in their hands, ran past them towards the colossal tower. Others hid in corners and shadows of buildings, frightened by the chaos.

Saul clenched his stomach as they walked. "Where are you taking us?"

Crooked Tooth, who seemed to be the leader of the group, turned his head and flashed the same menacing smile. "To Simon, of course. He'll know what to do with you."

"Who is Simon? Why would he want us?"

"What's wrong with you? Are your ears shot? I already told you. Greene has our men. We can trade."

"Why would Greene trade for us?"

"He takes an interest in outsiders."

They entered a vacant building. The rooms were filthy and rundown. As they walked down a set of stairs, the sunlight faded and darkness moved in. Crooked Tooth pulled a rod from his pocket and tapped the end. The tip illuminated, lighting the way. Vince and the others marveled at the sight. Light from nowhere. Like magic.

They continued along the path, and Vince noticed a flag hanging from the wall. In the center was a familiar image. A large tortoise climbing a pyramid. He nudged Saul. "Isn't that the Rodin crest?"

Crooked Tooth turned around. "What did you say?"

"Nothing. I said nothing."

The man glanced at the flag. "No. You said Rodin." He gazed deep into Vince's eyes. "What do you know about Rodin?"

Vince glared back. "Nothing. You misheard. May we continue?"

Crooked Tooth moved his gaze to Saul and the others, then turned around and kept walking. Saul shot Vince a look of concern, but said nothing.

They walked through a maze of underground hallways. Debris and dust occasionally fell as rumbles shook the ground above. They turned a corner and found themselves in an open room, illuminated only by a small glowing box at the center. The box displayed moving images behind the glass surface. More magic. A man's silhouette was cast upon the light. His back was facing them as he watched the images on the box.

"How do we look on television?" Crooked Tooth asked.

"Like terrorists," the man said without turning around. "We're heroes, but they always say we're terrorists."

Crooked Tooth walked to the side and started making a mug of tea. The ceramic mug had a picture of a turtle imprinted on the front. "There isn't much we can do about that, boss. They're too stubborn."

"No, there is something we can do. There must be a way to make them understand. I just haven't figured it out yet."

"I'm sure you will. You always do." He raised the mug to his lips and slurped the hot liquid.

"Enough flattery, Jonah. How is the charge going? Why are you down here? You should be on the front lines."

Jonah placed the mug down and walked up to the man. He leaned in and whispered into his ear.

The man finally turned around sauntered up to Vince. He had oily skin and rough stubble, and his hair was a wild mess. His eyes were wide and piercing. "So, tell me what you know about Rodin."

Vince held firm eye contact. "I already told your friend over there, we don't know what Rodin is. Never heard of it. He misheard us."

"I see. I'm a little disappointed, but if you say so, I have no reason to question you. We're all free to speak our minds here, right? As we always say, live free forever."

Vince flinched at the phrase.

"Ah, so you *do* recognize it. Of course, it would be familiar if you were from Rodin, but you've assured me that you never even heard of Rodin."

Saul stepped forward. "Who cares if we do or don't know about Rodin?"

The man smiled. "I care a great deal, actually."

"Yeah?" Saul said. "And who are you? Why are you so important?"

"I'm glad you asked. It is a very important question with an equally important answer. I am the face of the poor and forgotten, of the abused and cheated. An unsung hero of the City. I fight for freedom. For equality.

I lead because I can. Because no one else will. I follow in my father's footsteps and build from what my grandfather created. I lead the Crowns. I am Simon Hedcrown."

FIVE

VINCE AND SAUL both reacted when they heard the name Hedcrown. The name of the famous inventor from Rodin, who had ventured into the unknown, never to return.

"Yes," Simon said. "You heard correctly. I am a Hedcrown. I have Rodin blood."

"How is that possible?" Saul asked. "Harry Hedcrown left Rodin hundreds of years ago. He vanished into the flatlands. There's no way he could have survived."

"But he did," Simon responded. "Greene sent someone out to rescue him. A contact agent to bring him back to the City. And that's when he formed the Crowns."

"What are the Crowns?"

"We are the Crowns. We stand for freedom and fight against Greene. We strive to rescue every prisoner in his hold and provide them with the freedom they deserve. Live. Free. Forever."

Alan stepped forward. "I guess our goals align. We're here to stop Greene as well. We want to stop his tests and free all the test subjects." He stuck out his hand. "I think we got off on the wrong foot. We should be working together, not against each other."

Simon nodded. "If that's the case, I completely agree." He signaled for the others to lower their guns. "I apologize if Jonah frightened you. He can be a bit aggressive, but it's a good quality to have for an operation like this."

Jonah stood in the corner and watched them, leaning against the wall and sipping tea from his turtle mug.

"What's going on up there?" Ella asked. "The dust was crazy. I couldn't see anything. All I heard were explosions."

"Yes. We're charging the Spire. That's where Greene hides. The tall tower you probably saw when you came in. It's protected by three walls, each equipped with cannons.

"Cannons?" Rupert asked.

"You don't know what a cannon is?" He chuckled. "Wow, you guys really *are* outsiders." He pulled out his gun and held it up to show them. "Do you know what this is?"

"Yes," Vince said. "We encountered one earlier. It shoots thunder."

"Thunder? Ha! That's priceless. No, my friend. It shoots bullets." He opened the barrel and pulled one out. "These little metal balls. A cannon is a bigger version of this. About ten times as big."

"Holy crap!" Alan said. "I'd hate to run into one of those."

"Yes, they are very dangerous, but we counter them with our homemade bombs. That's how we took down the first wall."

"So you're just going in with brute force."

"That's really our only option. There's no way for us to sneak in." He paused for a moment, then pointed his finger towards Vince. "If you're from the outside, how do you know about Greene? How do you know about test subjects?"

Saul answered without thinking. "We *are* test subjects."

Vince glared at him. That was not information he wanted to share, not yet.

Simon stumbled back. "What? You're saying we have a group of escaped subjects?"

"Just Vince and I. The others are friends. And we didn't escape. They tested us outside of the City, without our knowledge."

"Fascinating. They have subjects in the outer world. What did they test?"

"We have the power to drain life from the living. Plants, animals, that kind of thing. It extends our life expectancy."

"Perfect!" Simon exclaimed. "You embody our motto. Live free forever. Two of Greene's prisoners defy his orders and live a free life. You represent everything the Crowns stand for. We need to spread the word. Make you the face of the Crowns." He turned to Jonah. "Make an announcement. We'll throw a rally tomorrow morning. That's where we'll introduce them to the people."

Jonah put down his empty turtle mug and left through the back door.

"Wait," Ella said. "We don't want to go around broadcasting our presence. We want to stay quiet. Catch Greene by surprise."

Simon shook his head. "There's no catching Greene by surprise. He has eyes everywhere. He already knows you're here, and I'm sure he knows we found you. We need to take advantage of the situation before he has time to react."

"How do you think he *will* react?" Rupert asked.

"I don't know, but there's no point in waiting to find out. What are your names?"

"Vince Vigo."

"Saul Shepherd."

"Rupert Howlett, and my falcon, Fred."

"Ella Weaver."

"Alan Trotter."

Simon glanced at them from a distance. "And you two are Greene's subjects." Vince and Saul nodded. "We need to get your names out there. Vince and Saul, the two who escaped Greene's hold and now live as free men. We'll have your faces on posters and television. Hell, I'll shout your names from the rooftops. By the end of tomorrow, everyone in the City will know who you are."

"This is a bit much," Saul said, "isn't it?" He was still clenching the pain in his stomach.

"Not at all. We must not squander this opportunity." Simon's eyes wandered down to Saul's stomach. "Are you hurt, friend? I see a lot of blood."

"I'm okay. I was shot earlier, but I'm healing up pretty well. I should be good to go in a couple of days."

"We'll get someone to look at it, just in case. We can't have the new face of the Crowns keeling over in pain. We need to show your strength. Your ability to overcome hardships and oppression."

"Believe me, I'm no role model. I'm not someone people should look up to. I've done things I'm not proud of."

"But you've changed," Vince said. "You've done so much good. You stopped Barnabus."

"Barnabus Carbul?" Simon asked. "You stopped him?"

Vince nodded. "Yes. He was the one watching us. I guess you could call him our contact agent. He went on a killing spree, but Saul put his life at risk to stop him. Barnabus is dead now."

Simon's surprised expression turned to joy. "I can't believe it. Carbul was on our top list of targets. You guys really *are* on our side. Fighting for the Crowns before you even know they exist."

"Barnabus was a monster. No one's going to miss him."

"Greene will certainly miss him. He was basically Greene's right-hand man."

"Really?" Ella asked. "He almost seemed scared of Greene."

"Everyone's scared of Greene, but some are closer to him than others. Barnabus was one of the guys that had been around forever. Many have come and gone, but he stuck by Greene's side. He was as loyal as anyone could be."

"A leader who rules with fear always fails," Rupert said. "Lead with love, that's what I always say."

"And you're one hell of a leader," Alan said. "Wouldn't have it any other way."

Simon continued with his original thought. "Regardless, we need to push you boys out into the public. Everyone in the City will know your names. Vince and Saul. The ones who live free forever."

A panicked Jonah entered the room. "Simon, we're losing too many men up there."

"Have we breached the second wall?"

"No, sir. They have too much firepower and our bomb supply is running low."

"Goddamn it! It took forever to make those bombs. I was certain it was enough to get through all three."

"I'm afraid not. We've barely even scratched the second wall. They're shooting us down like flies. It's a bloody mess out there."

Simon turned his back and mumbled to himself. He stomped the ground and punched the air, gritting his teeth and screaming obscenities. They all watched his tantrum build. His face grew red as he yelled even louder. His muscles clenched. His veins bulged from his neck.

After a few seconds, he gathered himself, regained his composure, and turned to face the others again. "I apologize. A lot of planning went into this operation. It is disheartening to learn that it was all for nothing."

Jonah tipped his hat. "Not for nothing, sir. We took down the first wall. They're more vulnerable than ever now."

"That is true. The first wall is down, but we have to move fast. Greene is sure to repair it quickly. If we sit around, we will lose our progress. We need to make more bombs. Jonah, tell the others to scavenge for materials."

Jonah began to leave.

"Wait. Is the rally ready to go?"

"We've announced a rally for tomorrow morning."

"Good. Now get moving."

Jonah left.

Simon turned back to Vince and Saul. "In the meantime, let me show you and your friends around."

Alan observed the room they were in. "No offense, but it doesn't look like there's much to show."

Simon chuckled. "Please. You haven't seen anything yet. Come, follow me." He clicked off the television and led them to the back. There was an empty hallway with a curtain at the far end. "When my grandfather founded the Crowns, it was just him and a few other people. His closest friends."

As they walked, they heard a rumble of people, growing louder from behind the curtain.

"He built a strong foundation with those people. They formed principles that made sense, that attracted others." They reached the curtain, and Simon grabbed the end. "He would smile if he saw how far we've come. How much we've grown." He pulled back the curtain to reveal a massive underground network of people.

They marveled at the sight. A series of tunnels holding hundreds of men, women, and children. People shuffled along, crowding the passageways. Salesmen stood at their booths, calling out prices as crowds passed by. Children pranced around a statue at the center of the square, chasing each other with innocent joy.

"Wow," Ella said. "There's a whole society down here. All of these people are against Greene?"

"Yes," Simon said proudly. "And this is only one of our bases. There are many more just like it, hidden throughout the City. Greene knows they exist, but he doesn't know we do business down here."

"There are so many people," she said. "How is Greene still in power if they all oppose him?"

"We are a large group, but we are still the minority. By quite a margin, actually. You've only seen a sliver of the City."

"That's amazing. It's so much bigger than Snow Peak."

"Snow Peak? Is that where you're from? Sounds cold."

They strolled along the path, weaving through the crowds of people. The tunnels were lit with the same magic Jonah had used, encapsulated in tall metal rods.

"What are those?" Alan asked.

"That, my friend, is a lamppost. I take it you've never seen electricity before? It powers the whole City. Greene has a generator in the Spire. He sends electricity all across the City. We may hate the guy, but it's damn hard to live with no lights."

Vince walked past the magic that had entranced the others. He was more interested in the statue that stood in front of them. The plaque underneath read:

Harry Hedcrown
Leader. Hero. Friend.

The statue itself was smeared with dirt and dust. Its bronze tint was hidden with black soot. The figure stood tall, displaying Harry in a triumphant pose.

Simon smiled with pride. "That's Grandpa. He was a hero."

Vince studied the features on his metal face. "I can't believe he made it out. He survived the flatlands."

"Barely," Simon said. "If the stories are true, he was on the heels of death when Greene's guy picked him up. I don't think he would have made it on his own."

"It was definitely rough," Saul said. "We wouldn't have made it without our powers."

Simon admired the sight of Vince and Saul standing together. "This is perfect. Our two new heroes, both from Rodin, following in Harry's footsteps. Surviving the flatlands and coming to the City to challenge Greene. I couldn't ask for a better setup. People are going to eat this up."

"We can't stay here for long," Vince said. "We need to focus on Greene."

Simon jumped with excitement. "Of course that's the goal, but your presence is important as well. What you represent is more damaging to Greene than anything you could do on your own. With the troops rallied, we'll form another attack. Take down the second and third wall. Then you can have Greene. But right now you need to motivate people. Men and women will die fighting for us. It's your job to inspire them. Give them something to fight for. Show them that freedom for their loved ones is possible. And once that third wall is down, we'll charge in and take control."

"There must be a better way," Ella said. "Brute force will only get people killed."

"It's a necessary sacrifice. The lives of our people are valuable, but the things Greene and his labbies do in the Spire are unforgivable. Cruel. Inhumane. All of those people in his lab were kidnapped. Some from the outside, but many from right here in the City. People disappear at night. He blames the growing criminal world, but we know it's really him. He sends people out at night and snatches us out of bed. Men. Women. Children." He took a moment to calm himself. Just thinking about it got him worked up. "The people sacrificing themselves to take down that wall? They *choose* to fight. They have a choice. They're fighting for their loved ones, a reward that's worth the risk."

"No, it isn't," Ella said. "It's not worth it if there's another way."

"There *is* no other way."

"There has to be." Her voice carried further as she grew agitated. "You can't just throw people at that wall like pawns. They're not disposable. Don't you care about them?"

"Of course I care." His voice also grew louder. "What do you think I'm fighting for? Without these people, the Crowns don't exist. I give them the freedom of choice, and they choose to fight by my side. I owe everything to them."

"Then don't throw their lives away like they're nothing!"

"Listen!" Simon yelled. "This is my operation. I've been doing this for a long time. I don't need some girl coming in and telling me how to run things around here."

Ella stepped forward, hot blood filling her cheeks. "What you need is—"

Rupert held her back and whispered in her ear. "This is neither the time nor the place. We can discuss this later amongst ourselves." He let her go, and she stepped back, pouting.

Simon could tell she was restraining herself. "Things have gotten a bit heated. Let's take some time to cool off. I am your host after all. Follow me. I'll provide you with beds."

SIX

S IMON SHOWED THEM their beds and left to plan for the rally in the morning. The beds were nothing special, but it beat sleeping in the snow plains. They unpacked their things and settled in.

Rupert approached Vince and Saul. "What do you think of this place? Can we trust them?"

Vince shrugged. "He speaks with passion. There's no doubt he wants to stop Greene. It's his approach that concerns me."

"Clearly Ella felt the same way," Saul said. "That was quite the little outburst you had back there."

She sneered. "The way he talks about people, like they're expendable. His brute force methods are careless. I don't like him."

Alan nodded. "Me neither."

Rupert nodded as well. "I feel the same way, but we must be careful how we act around here. Simon leads a strong group. A passionate group. In the right hands, they could be very useful, but with Simon in charge, they're dangerous. We should wait a bit longer. Think carefully about this. Maybe we can gain his trust. Get on his good side and steer the Crowns in the right direction."

"He already loves the two of you," Alan said, patting Vince and Saul on the back. "Two heroes born and raised in Rodin. Journeying across the flatlands and following in Harry Hedcrown's footsteps." He put his hands on his hips, stood in a triumphant pose, and spoke in a jovial voice. "A symbol of freedom!"

Ella laughed. "He was very enthusiastic about the two of you. We can use that to our advantage."

Vince nodded. "We can. We will make Simon happy and go to the rally tomorrow. Become the symbol he wants and gain his trust. Greene will surely see us if we go, but there is no getting around that. I suspect he already knows we're here anyway."

"There's no doubt he knows we're here," Saul said. "He's been watching us since day one. We killed one of his men and stole his boats. He's not dumb. He's been keeping a very close eye on us."

"We're not dumb either," Rupert said. "We'll be patient and make our moves carefully."

Alan struck down his fist. "And when the opportunity comes, we'll hit him where it hurts. For Patrick!"

They all repeated, "For Patrick."

SEVEN

CHARLOTTE WATCHED THE seconds on the clock tick away, waiting for the alert to end so she could get back to work. "How much longer do you think we'll be stuck in here?"

Trevor stuffed his mouth with food. "Who knows? Eat up. It could be a while."

She pushed her tray aside. "I'm not hungry."

"Suit yourself. More for me." He grabbed her tray and poured it onto his.

"You're such a pig."

"And I'm proud of it."

"This must be your dream. No work and enough food to last weeks."

"Add some television and I'd be in heaven."

"There is a television." She pointed over Trevor's shoulder.

He shook his head. "I mean real television. This is just the news."

"It's important that we know what's going on. Especially when the Crowns attack."

"Yeah, well, they're not attacking anymore. Greene could at least let us change the channel if nothing interesting is happening."

"Why are we still even in here? The Crowns backed off. We're not in danger anymore. We can get back to work."

Trevor's mouth was full of chicken. "They're just being cautious. We'll probably be in here until they secure that gap in the first wall. Why are you so anxious to get out of here? This isn't a punishment. It's not like they're going to lock us in here and suck out all of the air. Relax a little. Take advantage of this break."

"Vince and Saul are interesting to watch. I want to see where they are."

"Oh yeah, that's right. When this is all done, you get to go back and watch two of the most interesting people in the world. I have to watch people put on makeup."

Charlotte opened her journal to review Vince and Saul's recent activity.

Trevor watched her flip through the pages. "It's amazing, isn't it? Both of their lives, condensed into one little book."

She nodded as she turned to the very first entry. "These early ones aren't very thorough. Whoever had this job before me really slacked off."

"That's probably why they got canned. Greene doesn't put up with slackers. Cosmetic tests may be boring, but I'm thorough as hell with my reports."

"Keep at it and they'll promote you soon enough."

"That's the plan."

"Take advantage of the time you have right now. In my position, I get very little free time. There's always something important going on. You're single, right?"

Trevor nodded.

"Good. When you move up, you won't have time for dating, or a family. Your time will be fully dedicated to your subjects."

"You don't make it sound very glamorous."

"It isn't glamorous. Not even close. It's interesting, that's for sure, but it's also time-consuming and tedious. But when Vince and Saul die, because all test subjects eventually do, I'll be set for life. Greene will slap a paycheck down and I'll retire."

"It's ridiculous how much he pays everyone in the vitality sector."

"It's important to him. It always has been. From what I hear, he's a bit obsessed with discovering immortality. Living forever. There's a rumor going around that he's sterile, so he has no one to carry his legacy. Living for as long as possible is the next best thing. He's come a long way in achieving that. Three hundred years is a long time to live. People on the outside rarely make it to ninety. Not many people know that."

"I knew that. That's why the Hedcrown bloodline has such a quick turnaround. Harry was from the outside."

"Exactly. And that's why it's important to have subjects out there. We get more immediate results than we do in our labs. People die faster. That's imperative. To Greene, every wasted minute is one step closer to death."

"That's grim."

"It's also true. It means you don't waste time slacking off. If you do, death will sneak up and hit you like that." She snapped her fingers.

"I suppose that's true." He looked at the clock. "It's getting late. You going to bed soon?"

"I'll try to sleep a little, but safe room beds are never comfortable."

Trevor chuckled as he scooped the last bits of food from Charlotte's tray in his mouth. "This meal will knock me right out."

EIGHT

THE GROUP SLEPT well in the beds Simon provided. It was far better than any night in the snow plains. They all woke up refreshed and energized. As they got dressed, Simon entered with a man by his side.

"Good morning everyone," Simon said. "I hope the beds were to your liking."

Vince bowed his head. "They were very comfortable. Thank you for your hospitality."

"Only the best for our new heroes. The rally begins in a few hours. We'll get out there soon, but first, I brought someone to look at Saul's wound." He gestured to the man beside him. "This is Charles. He'll take care of any medical needs you require."

Rupert held up Fred. "This falcon is injured. Can you take a look at her as well?"

"Of course," Charles said. "Falcons are not my expertise, but I'll see what I can do. First, let me take a look at Saul." He walked over. "Show me your wound."

He lifted his shirt and revealed the scar. The red had faded to a normal flesh color.

"How recently did this happen?"

Saul laughed. "You're not going to believe me, but it was yesterday. I got shot by a gun."

"Yesterday, huh? So you have healing powers. You're one of Greene's vitality subjects."

"I guess, if that's what they call us." He was surprised by how casual he was.

"Any subjects assigned to healing, life extension, or just avoiding death in general, are supervised by Greene's vitality sector. It's his most valued sector in the Spire."

"That's right," Simon said. "I'm guessing the two of you are worth a lot to Greene. That's why turning you into icons is so important. We're going to twist his work around and have it bite him in the ass."

Charles examined the wound, pressing gently around the scar. "It looks like it's healing up well. Do you feel any pain?"

"Occasionally. Just a little."

"Give it a few more days. I suspect the pain will subside." He walked over to Fred, who was cradled in Rupert's arms. "Now let's take a look at this beauty." He stretched out her wing to see the wound. "There is a good amount of damage here. She won't be flying anytime soon. Have her take it easy for a while. Don't do anything strenuous. It will have to heal on its own."

"So just wait it out for both of them," Alan said.

"Essentially, yes. I apologize if this doesn't satisfy you. We don't have much equipment down here. Your conditions are not life threatening, and frankly, we're saving what we have for all of the injured from yesterday's attack."

Simon shook his head in shame. "We lost a lot of people yesterday, and countless were injured. Our supplies just can't keep up. We'll have to go on another supply raid soon, but until then, we'll make do with what we have."

Ella opened her mouth to argue against him, but saw Rupert's disapproving glare. Instead, she changed the subject. "What do you expect from the rally this morning?"

Simon smiled. "I'm glad you asked. It's important that we're all on the same page. It will be fairly simple. I've made it easy for you. I will start off by addressing the people with a speech. At that point, Vince and Saul will come up on stage and wave. If you wish to speak, you may, but you don't have to. My speech covers everything that needs saying. If you *do* choose to say something, make them words of inspiration. These people need all of the hope they can get."

"We prefer to stay silent," Vince said. "At least for now."

"Very well. Your presence will be enough to set off the crowd. I'm sure of it. There are a few last minute things I must deal with. I will come back to get you when it's time. In the meantime, relax. I'm sure you've all been through a lot."

He left the room, and Charles followed him out. Rupert held Fred up. "You hear that, girl? Relax. Let that wing heal."

She chirped in agreement.

Alan leaned back, kicked his legs up, and folded his arms behind his head. "If there's one thing I know how to do, it's relaxing. It sounds like Vince and Saul have all the work."

"You need to be vigilant as well," Vince said. "Simon seems confident that people will accept us, but we have no idea *how* they'll react. If something goes wrong, we need to be ready. The minute we lose our status as 'The Heroes from Rodin,' we become expendable. Simon will get rid of us. A man like him knows his goals, and if we challenge that in any way, he'll cut us loose."

Ella nodded. "It's clear, to him we're just tools. Just like all the people that charge to their death for him."

"It's true," Rupert said. "He is a man with good intentions, but his judgment is clouded." He glanced at Ella. "You need to keep those kinds of thoughts to yourself. At least for now. They could get us into trouble."

"Yes," she responded. "I understand how fragile the situation is."

"It's both fragile and crucial," Vince said. "Let's try to make it through this rally and see where it goes from there. If everything goes well, we'll be in a very good position."

"You guys will do fine," Alan said, still propped up on his bed. "You don't even have to talk. Just wave and let Simon do his thing."

"Even so," Vince said, "it's good to expect the worst. Things always go wrong when you least expect it."

NINE

THEY FOLLOWED SIMON into the courtyard, behind the stage. They could hear the rumblings of a large crowd on the other side.

Alan peered up at the tall buildings and open sky. "I thought the rally would be underground."

"No," Simon said. "This event is out in the open. We don't want to hide our heroes from Greene, we want to show them off." The crowd began to chant Simon's name. "I guess it's time. Stay down here. I'll call you up when the time is right. The rest of you stay put and enjoy the show." When he climbed up on stage, the crowd broke out in wild cheers. He raised his arms up and accepted the roar of the crowd.

Vince looked up at the giant monitors hanging from above, showing close-ups of Simon's face as he walked around.

"Their technology," Ella said, gazing up in awe. "It's amazing."

When the roar finally softened, Simon cleared his throat. "Thank you for coming on such short notice. It is a fine morning." His voice was amplified from large boxes hanging above the stage. "I would like to begin with a moment of silence for those that we lost yesterday. Please join me as we commemorate their sacrifice." He bowed his head. The people in the crowd did the same. "Thank you. Their loss was not without purpose. Thanks to their valiant efforts, we have broken through the first wall!" He threw his arms up in triumph. The crowd cheered.

"The wall has not fallen in over a hundred years. They said it was impossible. They said our efforts were hopeless. But yesterday, we proved them wrong. We've destroyed their first wall, damaged the second, and the third is within reach! Greene can hide in the Spire, but soon he will have to answer for his crimes. We will break in, free our loved ones, and stop Greene's reign!" The crowd cheered even louder.

Vince watched the charisma ooze from his skin. He had complete control of his audience.

"But our small victory does not mean we're done. It means the very opposite. We must fight harder while our enemy is hurt. Attack again while his defenses are scattered. It will be swift. It will be strong. It will strike fear into Greene's soul! I assure you all, victory is close. I can see it, and I know you can too. Now we just have to take it!"

The crowd broke out screaming. "Hedcrown! Hedcrown! Hedcrown!" Simon paced around with his arms up as the people called his name.

Alan stared at the close-up on the monitor. "Man, they really love this guy. They'd do anything for him."

Ella looked over. "That's the problem. With the right leader they could do so much, but instead, they follow a man who promises false hope."

When the crowd was quiet again, Simon continued. "I would now like to introduce you to two very important people. They joined our cause just yesterday. Vince, Saul, please come up on stage."

Vince and Saul stepped up. From here they could see the massive crowd. It was even larger than it sounded. Saul leaned over to Vince. "There are so many of them," he whispered.

"No need to whisper," Simon chuckled. "They can't hear you. I've got the microphone. Of course, when I'm done I'll hand it over if you want to say something." He raised the microphone back up to his lips. "These two gentlemen are very important. They come from—"

The hanging monitors cut to static. Simon stopped to see what was wrong. A curious mumble hummed from the crowd. Simon began to walk off stage, but the monitors flashed back on. They no longer displayed images of the stage. Instead, a close-up of a well-groomed man appeared. He wore a fitted suit with matching pants. His smile was both charming and infectious. The crowd heckled and yelled at his appearance.

"Greetings citizens," he said in a cheery voice, "This is Victor Greene, here to bring you some important news. I am proud to announce that, for the very first time in City history, we have visitors from the outside. This is a big event. It is something that will go down in the history books."

The crowd's disapproval grew louder. The monitor switched to the image of Vince and Saul standing on the stage, and then back to Greene.

"These two gentlemen, Vince Vigo and Saul Shepherd, are part of our research program. Volunteers from our vitality sector. Outliving their natural lifespan by over a hundred years, these two are shining examples of successful research subjects. They have come all this way to promote our thriving research program."

A roar of hate scattered amongst the people. They began throwing things on stage.

"With role model subjects like Vince and Saul, we are excited to pursue more opportunities, discover new possibilities, and make the world a better place. I would like to thank Vince and Saul for their participation and willingness to cooperate, and I personally welcome them to come visit us at the Spire. They have journeyed a long way, so be sure to welcome our new visitors. They are the pride of the Spire. This is Victor Greene. Have a wonderful day." The monitor cut to static and back to the stage.

Simon turned his back to the audience. "No! That bastard ruined everything!"

The crowd booed and hissed at the stage. Rocks and garbage came flying up. From the middle of the crowd, a voice screamed, "Get them! Kill them!" The people in front started climbing the stage.

"Come on!" Alan yelled. "What are you guys waiting for? Let's get out of here!"

Vince and Saul did not react. They stared at each other, frozen in place.

Alan threw his arms up. "What are they doing? We have to leave!"

Ella ran up and dashed to the center. She grabbed their arms and pulled them out of their daze. They ran off stage with the others as the ravenous mob followed. Ella led them down the street and around the corner. The steady roar grew as the mob got closer.

"What do we do?" Alan said. The desperation in his voice was palpable. "There's no way we can outrun them, and there's nowhere to go."

They all looked at each other with defeated eyes. They gathered close and joined hands, bracing themselves for impact. They closed their eyes as the mob washed over them.

Vince crouched as a man dove over him and toppled onto the pavement. A sea of arms pushed them together and pulled them apart. Vince struggled to keep hold of Rupert. A lady slammed into his shoulder and pulled him away.

"Saul!" he yelled. "Ella!" His voice was lost in the noise of the crowd.

They held him in place and tackled him to the ground. His heart raced as they struck his face and body. He closed his eyes and tried to focus. Control his breathing. Overcome the chaos. When he opened his eyes, a sack was pulled over his head and tightened. He could no longer see as they dragged him away. A sharp pinch shot pain up his arm. He grew nauseous and dizzy. His eyes began to drift. As he sunk into unconsciousness, the crowd disappeared.

An unknown voice whispered in his ear. "Don't worry, buddy. I've got you."

TEN

VINCE AWOKE IN a groggy state. His eyes fluttered, stinging with dryness. He was lying in bed, his head propped up by a pile of pillows. The walls were white and bare, and the checkered tile floor was spotless. To his side were machines stacked on top of each other, blinking and beeping with a rhythmic beat. Wires twisted out and attached to his arms, head, and chest. He pulled them off and tried to stand up. The machines blared a loud constant beep. He played with the buttons until the piercing sound stopped.

A young lady walked in holding a clipboard. "No, Mr. Vigo. You can't leave just yet. We have to keep an eye on you until the sedative wears off. Get back in bed."

"Where am I? Where are my friends?"

"Don't worry about your friends. They're all safe and sound. They're getting full body scans so we can treat any injuries from the rally. The Spire's treatment centers are the best in the City, so don't worry, you're all in good hands. My name is Margie, and I will be administering your body scan."

"The Spire? How did we get here? That mob, they had us."

The lady flashed a welcoming grin. "Fortunately for you, Mr. Greene has people undercover in the Crowns. They extracted all of you safely."

"But why? Why would Greene want to save us?"

"Why wouldn't he? Everyone here loves you. You're proof that our research matters. You're our success story. Vince and Saul, the boys who defied death and traveled from Rodin to meet Mr. Greene. What an inspiration. I imagine you must be excited to meet him. To shake the hand that granted you immortality." She laughed. "Of course, we all know it's not actually immortality. I'm sure you've figured that out by now. But it's fun to pretend. And it's pretty damn close."

Vince gave her a funny look. Did she know they were here to stop Greene? "Can I see my friends?"

"Not until we scan you. It is important that both you and Mr. Shepherd are at your healthiest." She turned the machines back on and placed the wires back on his skin. "Just sit back and I'll come get you when we're ready. And don't go messing with these machines again." She left the room and shut the door.

Vince peered out the window to a magnificent view of the City. He was dozens of floors up, at least, and could see the twisting maze of buildings fade into the distance. To the left, he saw the wall surrounding the City, and the gap they had entered from. Past the wall was the vast ocean. They had come a long way.

He was enjoying the view when the lady popped in. "Okay, Mr. Vigo. Come with me."

He followed her across the hall to another room. There was a large tube-shaped machine standing upright, slightly bigger than the size of a person.

She looked at her clipboard and scribbled some notes. "Please remove your clothes and step into the scanner."

Vince hesitated, staring at the contraption.

"I assure you, it won't hurt. You won't feel a thing."

He did as she said and removed his clothes. When he stepped inside, he saw glowing lights at his feet, around the edge of the tube.

"Please stand with your legs apart and your arms stretched out to the sides."

He followed her instructions.

"Now, stand still for a moment."

As he held his pose, a low hum grew louder. The lights at his feet grew brighter and spun around the outer edge. When they reached their full speed, they lifted up from the ground and slowly moved up his body. At the peak of the cycle, they stopped spinning and lowered back to the ground.

"See?" the lady said. "That wasn't so bad. You may put your clothes back on and I'll bring you to your friends. We will have the result of your scan tomorrow morning." He got dressed and followed her out. She led him to a waiting room area. "If you need anything else, anything at all, just give a wave." She turned around and left the room.

The others were sitting on long couches and talking amongst themselves. Saul looked up. "Vince! You're alright." He popped up and pulled him in for a hug. The others got up and joined in.

Vince saw Rupert's bare shoulder. "Where's Fred?"

"They're taking a look at her right now. They say they can probably treat her. Get her back to normal within a day or two. She just has to stay here overnight."

"That's good news. She seems to be in good hands. They have impressive medicine here."

"I've never seen anything like it. Certainly not in Snow Peak, that's for sure."

Vince looked at the rest of them "Did they scan you?"

"They insisted on scanning all of us," Ella said. "Wanted to make sure we're healthy. I guess Greene is looking out for us."

Saul shook his head. "I find that hard to believe."

"We shouldn't talk about this right now," Vince said.

"Why not?"

He shot a quick glance at the camera in the corner. They all saw.

"Because he's tired, Saul," Ella said in a casual voice. "He doesn't want to hear about your crazy conspiracy theories."

Saul looked down. "You're right. We're all tired."

"So what now?" Alan asked.

Rupert shrugged. "Can we leave? Where would we go?"

Just as the question left his mouth, a young gentleman entered the room. "Welcome to the Spire, friends." His voice was upbeat and cheery. "This is a very exciting day. Two subjects from the outside, coming all this way to support our program. It's amazing! Now, if everyone's ready, there is someone for you to meet. Follow me!"

ELEVEN

CHARLOTTE WATCHED THE screen as a recording of Simon's rally played. She snuck a quick glance at the door. Still locked. Trevor sat beside her, reading. She sighed. "I'm getting sick of this safe room."

Trevor turned the page. "Just relax. You work too hard."

"I can't relax. My two test subjects just became the most popular faces in the City. If anything, I should panic."

"Greene seems to have everything under control. If he needed you, he would have called—"

A voice blared from the loudspeaker. "Charlotte Marble. Please report to the briefing room. Repeat. Charlotte Marble. Please report to the briefing room."

She jumped from her seat and grabbed her journal. "Finally. I guess they need me after all." She walked to the door. "Enjoy the rest of your break."

He turned another page. "Don't worry, I will."

She pressed the button by the door, and it slid open. She wandered down the hall and took a left towards the briefing room. As she got closer, she heard a voice. It belonged to Greene. She had never met him before, but his voice was familiar. She had heard it so many times in his Citywide broadcasts.

When she reached the room, she turned the corner and glanced inside. There was a table full of well-dressed men and women. The men wore full suits and ties. The women wore business skirts and button-downs. They listened to Greene as he spoke at the head of the table.

He looked up. "Ah, just the person we were talking about. I take it you're Charlotte Marble."

She nodded. "Yes, I am."

"Very good." He turned to the others in the room. "Ms. Marble is Vince and Saul's monitor agent. I'm sure you've heard the news about your test subjects. It's all very exciting, isn't it?"

"It sure is." She entered the room and took a seat. "They've had one wild journey."

"It must be captivating to watch." He paused. "That is all for our meeting today. I would like to speak with Ms. Marble in private." The others gathered their things and shuffled out of the room. When they were gone, Greene took a seat across from Charlotte.

She adjusted her posture to look more professional. "It really is an honor to meet you, Mr. Greene."

"The pleasure is mine. It's always nice to meet one of my employees." He glanced down at her journal. "Could I see that? Do you mind?"

"No, not at all." She handed it over.

He flipped through the pages. "It really is amazing what those two have been through."

"It's amazing to watch."

"I can imagine so." He clapped the journal closed and handed it back. "You're a lucky one. Vince and Saul are front and center right now."

"The credit goes to you. Your broadcast is what made them popular."

He nodded. "I suppose that's true. It was necessary. You saw footage of the rally. You know Simon's intentions, right? He was going to do the same thing. Make those two a symbol, but for the Crowns. I had no choice. I had to turn his plan against him."

"I agree," she said, keeping firm eye contact with her employer. "It was the best move on your part."

"It was at the time, but now I'm stuck with another problem. A problem I'm sure you're aware of."

"They want to kill you."

"Correct. They didn't come here to support our program. They came to put a stop to it. They killed Barnabus. I'm next." He stood up and paced around the room. "You are their monitor agent. The only one who's seen the footage, other than me. Of course, I've only seen snippets. You have the whole picture, and everything you've seen is packed into that little journal of yours. Only you and I know the truth about them. We need to keep it that way. You cannot tell anyone what you've seen. You cannot show them your journal. If it gets out, it will cause a lot of trouble. Do you understand?"

A knot formed in her throat. She gulped and then nodded.

"Good. I have an assignment for you. I have transported Vince and Saul to the Spire. They are here right now. Their whole group. I would like you to give them a tour. Show them around. Take them to the labs, the monitor rooms, the safe rooms, anything. But keep an eye on them. I don't know what to do with them yet, but I'll figure something out. Maybe I can show them what the Crowns are really like. Get them on our side. I still have some planning to do, but in the meantime, I can't have them wandering on their own. I need you to watch them. Can you do that for me?"

"I'll do my best."

"Good. You can stay here. I'll send someone to get them." He walked to the door. "And try to be friendly. We want to make a good impression. Maybe we can change their minds. Show them all the good we do."

He left, leaving Charlotte alone, waiting patiently at the head of the table.

TWELVE

Vince and the others followed the young gentleman. "You'll all love it here in the Spire," he said as he guided them through a maze of halls. "We have a lot of impressive stuff to show off, and it's all thanks to volunteers like you. You help us make the City a better place." He turned the corner and led them into a room.

A woman sat at the head of the table. She stood up and extended her hand. "Hello! My name is Charlotte. It is so good to finally meet you in person. I will be giving you a tour of our facilities."

"Nice to meet you," Vince said. "I'm Vince. This is Saul, Ella—"

"Please, no need for introductions. I already know all of you."

"How?" Rupert asked.

Charlotte gripped her journal, concealing it behind her back. "Mr. Greene briefed me beforehand. He was very thorough."

"Speaking of Greene," Alan said, "where is he? When that guy said we were meeting someone, I assumed he meant Greene."

"Unfortunately, Mr. Greene is busy at the moment. He couldn't be here himself, but he assigned me to show you around. I can get all of you familiar with what we do here in the Spire. Shall we get started?" She led them out of the room.

As they walked, Alan examined the walls. "These hallways are so…blank."

"We like to keep a clean look to our facilities. Hallways, labs, even our bathrooms."

"What do you do in the labs?" Rupert asked.

"That's a good question. And that happens to be our first stop."

She pushed through a set of double doors that read *Testing Labs*. They opened up to a glass hallway. The walls on each side were floor to ceiling windows. Beyond the glass were small rooms. Some were dark and empty. Others were occupied by two or three people, whose clothes were torn up rags covered in dirt. They looked weak and ill.

Ella stared at a skinny old man through the glass, shivering in the corner by himself. "Why are they all so weak?" she asked. "Are all of your subjects like this?"

"Not at all. This is the rehabilitation sector. Every so often, we find someone from the outside world who is in critical shape. This is where we help them recover."

Ella took a closer look. The man was quivering back and forth.

Charlotte continued walking. "We have various sectors that study different areas of research. As you may have heard, the two of you are part of the vitality sector."

"Vitality," Saul repeated.

"Yes. The rehabilitation and medical sectors are branches of our Vitality sector. It is Mr. Greene's most valued sector. We experiment with ways to extend the human lifespan. To avoid death."

"Nobody can avoid death," Rupert said.

"These two here have done quite a good job of avoiding death actually. The average lifespan of a human from the outside is sixty years. In Rodin, it's eighty. How long have you two lived?"

"Just about two hundred years," Saul said.

"I'd call that a success. Wouldn't you?"

"It is impressive," Rupert said, "but everyone dies eventually. That's just a part of life."

"Well, Mr. Greene is trying to change that. We make progress every day. We've also made breakthroughs in transportation, medicine, cosmetics, food, defense, and the list goes on. I can show you one of the other sectors later on. The Spire is split up by floor, so each floor is identical, for a different sector. Now that you've seen some of the labs, I can show you a monitor room."

They followed her out of the labs. "Monitor room?" Ella asked.

"Yes. Every patient is assigned a monitor agent. They all observe their subjects through cameras. The monitor room is exactly what it sounds like. It's full of monitors that help the agent track their subject. Some monitor agents have multiple subjects, but a big case like Vince and Saul is a full-time deal."

"So they watch their subjects all day? That's it?"

"For the most part. Of course, they get time to eat and sleep. Whenever they aren't watching, they're recording the footage so they can watch later. They keep track of everything in a journal. If anything important happens, they write it down and report it directly to Mr. Greene. It's a hard job that takes a lot of commitment, but big cases pay a lot. Most monitor agents retire after their first big case."

Vince looked at the cameras all around them. "So who is our monitor agent?"

"Yeah," Saul said. "If they've watched us for two hundred years, their pay must be crazy."

Charlotte hesitated. "I'm not sure who your monitor agent is, but I'm sure their getting compensated quite well." She pushed through another set of doors. "This is a monitor room."

The walls were stacked with dozens of screens, most showing footage of the labs they were just in. The bright aura of light from the monitors made the room glow an unnatural color.

Alan entered and sat in the empty chair. "There's no one here. Where is everyone?"

"You probably heard about the attack we had yesterday. The Crowns were bombing our walls. All employees in the Spire are instructed to stay in their safe rooms until everything is safe. My guess is they want to secure the hole in our first wall before letting people out."

"You have safe rooms?" Rupert asked. "What kind of things do you keep there?"

"All of the necessities. Preserved food, beds, that kind of stuff. There are televisions for the news to keep us all updated. And if things get really bad, the safe rooms are located on the back side of the building. We have evacuation pods that shoot out over the City wall and into the ocean."

"Have you ever used those?" Alan asked.

"The evacuation pods? Only for drills. We've never had to use them for a real emergency, but it's good to know it's an option if something goes wrong. Especially with all of these terrorist attacks lately."

"Can we see them?" Vince asked. "The safe rooms?"

She shook her head. "Unfortunately, they are currently being used. We're not supposed to open them while an alert is in effect. However, once the alert is over, I would be happy to show you our safe rooms."

Saul walked up to the desk and picked up the journal that was lying face down.

"Please," Charlotte said. "You shouldn't be reading that. All monitor agent journals are confidential. This agent shouldn't have left it behind."

"These entries are so detailed," Saul said as he flipped through. "There's an entry for every day."

"Rehabilitation subjects are usually under closer watch. They require constant supervision. Subjects like you and Vince don't require as much detail. Only the highlights. Now please put down that journal."

Saul listened, and laid the book down on the desk how he found it. "We've definitely seen some *major* things, that's for sure."

She chuckled. "Believe me, I know."

Vince studied her reaction. "What exactly *do* you know about us? What did Greene brief you on?"

She pondered the question, thinking very carefully of how to answer. "I know that you volunteered as subjects when you were boys. I know that your case was such a success that you wanted to come to the City to thank Mr. Greene in person."

"That just about covers it," Alan said. "Here to meet the man himself. Victor Greene. The man who gave them immortality."

Charlotte locked eyes with Vince. He was watching her very closely. She broke eye contact and glanced at her feet. "Of course, everyone here in the Spire is ecstatic about your visit. There's nothing like a great success story to boost everyone's mood. People will be lining up to shake your hands. We don't get many visitors from the outside."

Ella looked up and down the halls. "I don't see anyone here to see us. In fact, only three people have spoken to us since we got here."

"It's hard while the Spire is still under alert, but Mr. Greene may hold a conference to introduce you in person. He might even broadcast it across the City. His first broadcast was so well-received; the people of the City would love to see more."

"Really?" Ella said. "They seemed pretty set on killing us yesterday."

"Those weren't normal City goers. They were Crowns. Terrorists. Violent people who act on impulse and hurt innocent people to get what they want. Trust me, you don't want their approval."

"When exactly will we get to meet Greene?" Saul asked. "We've come all this way. He must be a busy man, but surely he can put aside a few minutes to meet us."

"I promise, you'll meet him. Though it's hard to say when exactly. We will have to wait for his call, but in the meantime, I'll stay with you. I can show you around some more if you'd like. We could stop by one of the other sectors. Perhaps the food sector to do a little taste test."

"I presume Greene intends for us to stay here overnight," Vince said. "Can you show us to our beds? It has been quite an exhausting day."

"Of course," she said cheerfully. "Follow me." She brought them to a room with five beds. "I believe this room is yours."

Their bags sat on each of their beds. Rupert picked through his things to see if anything was missing. "How did you get these?"

"We have agents undercover in Simon's base. The same ones that rescued you grabbed your bags as well."

"We really owe them one," Alan said. "If it wasn't for them, we'd be dead."

"You owe Mr. Greene one. He is likely the one who gave the order."

"Of course," Vince said. "We will make sure to show our gratitude when we finally get to meet him."

"I assure you it will be soon. He is a busy man, but he keeps his priorities straight. You two are right up there on his list."

"Thank you for showing us around. If you don't mind, we would now like some privacy."

Charlotte bowed. "Yes, of course. I'll just be over here in the corner. Don't mind me."

Saul squinted at her. "I think he meant to ask for you to leave."

"I apologize. Mr. Greene has asked me to stay with you. The Spire can be an overwhelming place, and you are not yet familiar with our technology. We wouldn't want you to get lost." She wandered over to the corner and leaned against the wall. "I'll just be over here, out of your way. Feel free to rest. I'll let you know when Mr. Greene is ready to see you."

The group turned their backs to her, huddling around their bags, pretending to ruffle through them.

"What do you think of her," Vince whispered. "She seems a little off. The way she's acting. I think she's hiding something from us."

Ella nodded. "I agree. I think she knows more about us than what she says."

"So what should we do about it?" Alan asked. "We can't prove she's lying. And even if we could, there's still nothing we can do about it."

Rupert eyed her as she sat in the corner. She pulled out a journal and started flipping through the pages. "I don't think we can trust her."

Charlotte looked up. "You know, you don't have to whisper. Sure, there are cameras everywhere, but they can't hear you."

"What?" Rupert asked.

"They can't hear you. There are no microphones. The cameras are for security, but microphones breach our privacy policy."

"You're still here," Alan said. "Not that we're hiding anything from you. We were just talking as a group."

"I didn't mean to interrupt," she said. "Just thought you should know. Carry on." She buried her face back in her journal.

"What is that?" Saul said. He walked over to Charlotte.

"What is what?" She said as she shuffled the journal behind her back.

He grabbed it out of her hands and read the words on the cover. "Monitor Journal: Project Lazarus." He flipped to a random page. "Barnabus has made first contact. It went poorly. He has injected Saul. Vince remains clean. Barnabus has sustained a stab wound to the eye. He is returning to the City. The boys are preparing for school. Will monitor Saul closely to see the effects of the formula." He looked to the group, and then back to Charlotte. "This is the day we met Barnabus. Why is this in here? Why do you have this?"

Vince stepped forward. "She's our monitor agent."

She stared at the journal in Saul's hands. "Yes, I am your monitor agent."

"That's how you know so much about us," Vince said.

"Correct."

"You know everything about us," Saul said. "You know why we're really here."

Charlotte leaned in. "You have to keep this to yourself. If Greene finds out that you know, I'm in big trouble." Her eyes wandered to the cameras scattered throughout the room. She panicked and plucked the journal right out of Saul's hands. "They can't hear us, but they can see us." She tucked it behind her back. "I just hope he didn't see you reading it."

"You seem scared of him," Ella said.

"Scared is the wrong word. I'm intimidated by him. He is a powerful man. Rarely does anyone get to meet him up close. Today was my first time. The one thing he asked of me was to keep what I know about you to myself. Only Greene and I know the truth. Everyone else in the Spire thinks you're here to thank Greene, not kill him. I'm the one loose end in his plan to fool the City. That puts me under a lot of pressure."

Vince saw the genuine stress in her eyes. "I see. We have certainly put you in a tough position, and for that, I apologize. We still intend to stop Greene, but your secret is safe with us."

Her tense shoulders relaxed. "Thank you. You can trust me. I won't report anything to Greene."

"What now?" Alan asked

Vince shrugged. "What does Greene have planned for us? Do you know?"

"I've told you as much as I know. He is planning a conference of some kind. I presume that's when he will show you off to the Spire. He's transforming the two of you into objects of pride. Something the Spire can look up to. As far as I know, that is ultimately his goal. He does not wish to kill you. He wants to recruit you to fight against the Crowns."

"Why would we help him?" Saul asked. "He's given us nothing but heartache."

"He has put you through a lot, but you've seen the Crowns. You know how violent they can get."

"It's because of Simon," Ella said.

"Exactly. They are led by a savage man. One who leads them only further into savagery. Greene may have done bad things to you, but Simon is much worse."

"Sure, he was a bit strange," Alan said, "but he can't be worse than Greene."

She shook her head. "You don't understand. He's much worse. Let me show you."

THIRTEEN

CHARLOTTE BROUGHT THEM to her own monitor room. The screens displayed images from Vince and Saul's past. Their life in Rodin as children. Their trek through the flatlands. Their encounter with Barnabus. It was all there. The screen in the center showed the six of them standing in the monitor room. She chuckled and looked up at the camera above the door. "I guess I don't need this anymore." She flipped a switch, and the screen turned blue. She opened a drawer underneath the desk. "These are Simon's records." Hundreds of little cartridges were lined up in rows, each labeled with dates and times. She browsed through, running her fingers along the labels as she read them. "I believe this is the one." She pulled out a single cartridge and pushed it into a slot below the screen.

An image popped up. It was Simon. He was pacing back and forth in front of a group of Crowns, presumably giving a speech, but there was no sound to hear his word.

"So what?" Alan said. "He's just giving a speech. Getting them excited."

"Keep watching."

Another man walked into frame and tapped him on the shoulder. He leaned in and whispered something into his ear. Simon stopped, glared at the man, and then started to yell. He stomped the ground and threw his arms in a fit of rage. His entire face turned bright red. He drew his gun, pointed it at the man's head, and fired. The other men did not react. They stood in formation and awaited orders. Simon swung the gun around at one of them and pulled the trigger. Moved to the next. Pulled the trigger. His men stood still as the gun moved down the line."

"What?" Ella said, confused. "Why is he killing his own people?"

"He was throwing a fit, simple as that. It was the day we reclaimed one of our supply posts. He had captured it from us just days earlier. That man was giving him the bad news. He killed twelve of his men that day."

"He's nuts."

"He has a temper for sure." She popped the cartridge out. "I have more." She picked out another one and slipped it in.

Another image came up. This one was in some sort of store. It was a large warehouse with shelves full of products. People walked up and down the aisles, browsing through the selection. A group of armed men and women charged in, Simon leading in front. They yelled at customers and forced them to the ground. He said a few words and then signaled to his troops. They pointed their guns and fired. Simon left and returned with jugs of gasoline. They drenched the aisles until they were all out, and then lit the place on fire.

"Jeez!" Alan said.

"It's savage, I know," Charlotte said. "This was a store that Greene owned. There are many of them throughout the City. Lots of people shop there because it's affordable. To Greene, it's important that everyone has food and water, even those struggling with money, so he provides low-cost options. But to Simon, anyone who shops at these stores is a supporter of Greene. He kills them because he believes they're against his cause. In reality, they are only trying to put food on their tables. Innocent people die every week because of this."

"He does this a lot?" Rupert asked.

"All the time. This was just one instance, but he's attacked a number of Greene's stores throughout the City. He's slaughtered peaceful supporters of Greene. Unarmed people who want to support what we do."

"I'm starting to get the picture," Alan said. "This Simon guy is bad news."

Charlotte reached back into the drawer. "I have one more to show you." She pushed in another cartridge.

A little girl stood alone in an alley. Simon walked into frame holding a large gun. He handed it over to her and walked back out. When he returned, he was dragging a man. The man was tied up, gagged, and blindfolded. Simon dropped him in front of her and pointed at his head. The girl refused, shaking her head. Simon burst out yelling. She teared up, the gun trembling in her hand. She raised it up, closed her eyes, and shot. The man's head exploded, and his body fell to the ground. She stared at the headless corpse in terror. Simon took the gun from her, patted her head, and walked out.

"I think we've seen enough," Ella said.

Charlotte nodded. "I know it's hard to watch. Simon recruits kids at a young age. Forces them to kill. Greene has a strict no-children policy. He doesn't recruit children as soldiers, and they must give their consent to be test subjects." She looked at Vince and Saul. "Of course, you two are the exception. Barnabus panicked and disobeyed orders. He was not meant to inject you against your will. He was punished for that."

They were all silent as they walked back to their bedroom. When they arrived, Rupert turned to Charlotte. "Do you mind if we talk amongst ourselves for a moment?"

She nodded. "Of course. Take all the time you need."

They huddled in the corner. "What do you think?" Alan asked. "Simon seems like a pretty bad guy."

Rupert nodded. "I agree. Greene may be bad, but Simon is a cruel human being. Cruel and out of his mind. Those two things don't go well together."

"I knew it from the moment we met him," Ella said. "He's no good. He needs to be stopped."

Rupert turned to Vince and Saul. "What do you two think?"

Vince looked at Saul, and then back at the others. "It's true, we came here to stop Greene and that has not changed. But he's not going anywhere. I think we can all agree that Simon is far worse. Every day he's out there, innocent people die. The Crowns have a noble cause, but they're misguided. They need a good leader, and Simon is the opposite of that. He is a virus that has infected them and turned them into terrorists. Greene can wait. Simon needs to be stopped right away."

He glanced at Saul for approval. Saul nodded. "I'm right there with you, buddy."

"So we all agree," Rupert said. "What is our next course of action?"

"It sounds like Greene is welcoming us with open arms," Alan said. "He's making the two of you the *Pride of the Spire*. He's already using us to hurt Simon. I say we play along. Team up with him. Once Simon's out of the picture, we can turn on him and catch him by surprise."

"Do you think we can trust him? He knows so much about us. He knows why we're *really* here."

"He can't kill us," Vince said. "He needs us. He needs our image. If he kills us, the people will be outraged."

"So we all agree," Ella said. "We cooperate with Greene to take out Simon."

They all nodded and broke their huddle.

Rupert walked over to Charlotte. "We'll help stop Simon. We'll do whatever Greene asks."

"Wonderful! Greene will be pleased to hear that. I will let you know when he is ready to see you. In the meantime, get some rest. I know you've all been through a lot."

Alan fell onto one of the beds. It was the most comfortable thing he had ever laid on. "Damn right. I'm beat."

Ella walked to the bed next to him. "Sleep sounds nice." She looked up. "Are you going to watch us?"

Charlotte nodded. "Sorry, I have to. It's my job."

"You can take a break," Alan said. "We won't tell."

She looked at a camera in the corner. "They're watching, remember? Rest well, We're sure to be busy for the next few days." She opened her journal and began a new entry. *Vince and Saul arrive at the Spire.*

FOURTEEN

VINCE WOKE UP to the sound of a blaring voice. It was coming from the loud speaker.

"Charlotte Marble. Please escort our guests to the briefing room. Repeat. Charlotte Marble. Please escort our guests to the briefing room."

Charlotte stood up. "It's time. I guess Greene is ready to see you."

"Finally," Alan said as he got out of bed. "We've already been here a whole day."

"He must have something big planned for you. He was planning all day yesterday. Are you ready?" They nodded. "Okay, follow me."

They walked through the halls, past the rehabilitation labs again. This time, there were not only test subjects, but people in long white cloaks as well. Their uniforms bore the same City crest that was plastered on everything else. The camera. The boat. They had seen it everywhere.

"Looks like the alert has been lifted. The labbies are back to work." The workers in white observed their subjects, writing down notes in a journal similar to Charlotte's. "Let's go. We don't want to keep Greene waiting."

They passed through the double doors and back towards the briefing room. Saul nudged Vince. "What do you think he's like?" he whispered.

"I don't know, but we're about to find out."

Charlotte looked back. "Relax. It's true he's a powerful man, but he likes you. You'll be fine."

They turned the corner and entered the briefing room. A man sat at the head of the table. He stood up and opened his arms. "Welcome friends." His voice was deep. "It's so good to finally meet you in person. I am Victor Greene." He stuck out his hand to shake theirs. His grip was firm. "Now I know you have a lot of questions, but that will have to wait just a little longer while I speak with Ms. Marble. In the meantime, make yourselves comfortable."

He pulled Charlotte aside and lowered his voice. "Excellent work Ms. Marble. Showing them footage of Simon was a brilliant idea. Just what we needed to get them on our side. Did it work?"

"I think so."

"Fantastic. You have done well. I'm going to keep you with them. There is no need to watch them on a screen when they're here in person, right?"

"I suppose that's true, sir."

"From now on, you are their escort. You will show them around and bring them wherever they need to be. But secretly, you will continue to observe them. Note anything of interest in your journal. Do everything you do in the monitor room, but in person. And if they start to have doubts, you can nudge them in the right direction."

"Yes, sir."

"Very good." He turned around to address the others. "Sorry to keep you waiting. I know you were eager to meet me. I have certainly been eager to meet you. People around here call me Mr. Greene, but let's move past formalities. Please, call me Victor. Now let's get to business. It appears that we have a common goal. You met Simon, correct?"

"Yes," Saul answered. "That's correct. He seemed okay when we met him. We had no idea he was so...so..."

"Vicious?" Victor said. "Cruel? Savage? Barbaric? There are many words to describe him, but none of them quite capture his essence. He's an evil man guided by false justice. He disturbs the peace in the City that I work so hard to achieve. He's killed countless numbers of innocent people in the name of his so-called justice. But how can that be justice? It can't. I don't have to convince you. You've already seen it. The Crowns don't only follow him, they worship him. They believe he is the solution to all of their problems, and that if he takes down the Spire, pain and sorrow will disappear. But it won't. It will only spread chaos. Pain and sorrow will always be present, but here in the Spire, we try to make life a little better for everyone.

"Our tests help many people. Your very own vitality injection has led to some great breakthroughs in life expectancy. Simon looks past all of the good we do and focuses on false accusations. He antagonizes us. Turns the people against me when I'm only trying to help. He is a virus. An infection that grows in the form of the Crowns and attacks our peaceful society. He needs to be eliminated. Taken out. Exterminated."

He pointed to Vince and Saul. "That's where you two come in. He was going to make you the face of the Crowns. I plan on doing the exact opposite. You will be a success story for the Spire. A triumph for the people of the City to look up to. A shining example of why we do these tests."

"And what do *we* do?" Alan asked.

"Support them. They'll need all the support they can get. There are going to be conferences and meet ups. We'll get the two of you out into the public. Meet people face to face. Vince and Saul will be all-stars, and being all-stars is a lot of work. They'll need good friends by their sides."

"That sounds like a lot of work," Saul said.

"It will most definitely be a lot of work, but I assure you it will not be in vain. Your hard work will bring us closer to our goal. It will help tear Simon down from his throne. We will ease you in with the conference. You don't have to say anything. Just show up, stand on stage, and let me do the talking. We'll take it from there."

"When is the conference?"

Victor looked at his watch. "In about twenty minutes. I spent all night planning it. I've opened it up to all Spire employees, as well as the media. Your story will be broadcast across the City."

"Isn't this all a bit fast?" Ella asked. "We only just got here yesterday. Can't we have some time to rest?"

"There is no time to rest. Simon attacked us and he did a lot of damage. We managed to ward him off, but with our first wall down and our defenses scattered, he is bound to attack again, and soon. There's no way he would give up this opportunity. We have to hurt him before he can hurt us. This conference will boost the morale of our people and hopefully convert some of the Crowns."

"And if it doesn't?" Rupert asked.

"Then it doesn't. No harm done. It will still help my employees feel good about their work." He looked at his watch again. "We should make our way to the auditorium. We don't want to keep them waiting. Ms. Marble will show you the way. I need to make some last minute preparations, but I will see you up on stage." He walked to the door and turned around. "You'll all do great. I know it. Let's hit Simon where it hurts." He turned his back and left.

Charlotte studied their faces. "What do you think? Is he what you expected?"

Alan shook his head. "He was a lot nicer than I thought he would be."

"He was very enthusiastic about his plans for us," Vince said. "Simon was the exact same way."

"Trust me," Charlotte said. "Greene and Simon are not alike. They're opposite ends of a spectrum, and it looks like you're caught in the middle. You may have your doubts about Greene, but in this fight, you want him to win. Like he said, the City in Simon's hands would be chaos. Many people question the tests we do here, but Simon is the wrong person to lead those people."

"That's why we're helping you," Ella said. "You already know we don't support the tests, but Simon needs to be stopped."

"And he will be," Charlotte said. "Greene is a powerful man with the drive to achieve the impossible. If he wants Simon gone, it'll happen. He always gets what he wants."

FIFTEEN

THEY STOOD BACKSTAGE waiting for the conference to begin. There was a hum of chatter coming from the other side.

"Well this feels familiar," Alan said. "First Simon, now Greene. People really want to make you guys famous."

"With good reason," Rupert said. "I take it most people around here don't see outsiders very often. Vince and Saul have a connection with Harry Hedcrown. And they're successful test subjects. They serve as role models for both sides."

"I know that, but we've been here only two days, and we've already been to two of these things. At this rate, the whole world will know Vince and Saul by the end of next week."

Rupert ignored him. "I'm actually quite curious to see how this crowd reacts. It will most likely be positive, but how positive? They seem more reserved than the crowd at Simon's rally."

"That's a good thing," Vince said. "We don't want to fight through another angry mob. We got lucky last time, but if *this* crowd turns on us, we won't have Greene to save us. In fact, if things go wrong, he'll have every reason to kill us."

"Well that puts my mind at ease," Saul said. "I didn't realize our lives depended on this conference."

"It very well may. We must be very careful how we handle this."

"Greene wants you to succeed," Ella said. "He wants the crowd to like you, so just let him do all of the talking. Don't say a single word up there."

Vince nodded. "I agree. We'll stand up there, let Greene introduce us, and hopefully that will be enough."

"And if it isn't?" Alan asked.

"Then I guess we'll have to say something," Saul answered.

"Remember," Vince said. "Greene knows why we're really here, but the people of the City don't. They think we look up to him, admire him. We have to act as if we do. Put on a show. If they doubt our relationship with Greene for even a moment, our lives are at risk. Greene is powerful and dangerous, but as long as we have the people on our side, he can't touch us."

The lights of the auditorium dimmed. The low hum of chatter faded. A voice projected from above. "The conference is about to begin. Please refrain from talking during the presentation. There will be time for questions afterward. Now please welcome your fearless leader, Mr. Victor Greene."

A light applause spread across the floor and dissipated as Greene took the stage.

"Thank you all for coming on such short notice. We have some big news here in the City, which I'm sure you have already heard. But before we get to that, I would like to go over the Spire's test output for the year. We have had a good one. Performance is at an all-time high, and we're seeing more test subjects than ever before. This will help us pave a path to a better future for the City. Our cosmetic sector has innovated in exciting ways, advancing in cosmetic surgery and artificial enhancements. With surgery, we can now look exactly how we want. There are a few minor flaws that we are ironing out, but once development is complete, people will have exciting opportunities in the world of beauty.

"In our defense sector, we have enhanced our evacuation pods. They are now faster and safer than ever before. With the attacks from Simon, we have made our safety procedures in the Spire a priority, so that you can feel safe while you work. You all experienced our lockdown exercise the other day, and you did a wonderful job at following protocol. Everyone was safe and secured in their designated safe rooms, just as planned. Your compliance is much appreciated. As you all know, the first wall has fallen, but I don't want you to worry. We have assessed the damage and aim to build it back up even stronger than before. We will fortify the wall to ensure that Simon never breaks through it again. Our tested cannons proved a great success in driving his forces away. This is all thanks to the head of our defense sector, Dean Morton. We are working closely with him to develop an even stronger version of the cannon. We will keep you updated as more news comes.

"And finally, the big news from our vitality sector. Mr. Vigo. Mr. Shepherd. Please come on stage." Another light applause began as they walked up to join Greene. "As you have heard in my broadcast the other day, these two boys…well, they're not boys anymore…these two gentlemen have come from the outside world, all the way from a place called Rodin. They volunteered as test subjects over two hundred years ago, and now they have journeyed to the City to thank me. To thank us. The Spire has given them the opportunity to live past death. This is a shining example of the great things we can achieve. Our tests help better the world. We are not the monsters Simon makes us out to be. We have one goal in mind, and that is to help the people. These two are living proof that we can succeed. Please join me in welcoming our new friends."

He clapped his hands, and the crowd joined along. The applause grew, as people cheered and whistled. Ella, Alan, and Rupert cheered from backstage with the rest of them. Vince and Saul smiled and waved, peering out at the massive crowd, shocked by the overwhelmingly positive response. Perhaps this would be easier than they thought.

When the applause died down, Greene continued. "It truly is a great time for the Spire. The future looks bright for our people." He turned to Vince and Saul. "Before I take questions from the audience, do either of you want to say anything?"

Vince began to respectfully decline, but a voice echoed from the crowd. "Speech!" The single voice was joined by others as they started to chant. "Speech! Speech! Speech!"

Greene chuckled. "It looks like they want a speech."

Saul reached for the microphone, looking to Vince for approval. He nodded. With the microphone in hand, Saul moved to the center of the stage. "I will say a few words. We have come—"

"Sorry," Greene interrupted. "Please hold the microphone up so these fine people can hear you."

Saul raised his hand. "As I was saying, we have come a long way. We've crossed deserts and traversed snow plains. We've sailed oceans and climbed mountains. And we did all of it to thank this man." He pointed to Greene. "He is a generous man who has bestowed a gift upon us, and we are eternally grateful. We've been through a lot, and we've seen many things, but the City and the Spire have struck us with awe. Nothing compares to the monumental achievements that you have accomplished. All of you do great work. You change lives. You make them better. The City would not be the same without you."

He handed the microphone back to Greene, and the crowd erupted. They stood up and cheered and waved their arms around. People in the front row lifted up cameras to snap pictures of Saul as he waved.

Greene clapped along with the audience. "I couldn't have said it better myself. Inspiring words from our new visitor. You two truly are the pride of the Spire. Once again, I would like to thank all of you for coming to this conference. These are exciting times and I see bright things ahead of us. I will open it up for questions now."

People stood from their seats and lined up at the microphones that were in front of the stage.

The first person to ask a question was a young woman. "This question is for Mr. Vigo and Mr. Shepherd. Where is Rodin? How far have you traveled to get here?"

"That is a very good question," Greene said. "I suppose we should get extra microphones. I predict most of the questions will be for you, not me." He waved to a person off stage who came up and handed each of them their own microphone. "Now that the audience can hear you, would you like to answer the question?"

"Of course," Saul said. "Rodin is a place very far from here. Almost a lifetime away. We have been traveling since we were young boys, leaving Rodin over two hundred years ago. We took breaks only when we needed to. And we walked the whole way. Thinking back, I am shocked at how far we've come. We left as young boys, and we only just arrived, two hundred years later."

"Why would you travel so far? Is it really just to thank Mr. Greene?"

"He is the reason we could make the journey in the first place. Without him, we would have died a long time ago. He has granted us life. We are eternally indebted to him. We support the work he does, and if he can give more people what he gave to us, we want to do everything we can to help him."

"Thank you." The woman stepped away.

Alan nudged Ella as they watched backstage. "Saul's pretty good at this. He knows exactly what Greene wants to hear. Vince, on the other hand, hasn't said a word."

"I don't think Vince is much of a public speaker," She said. "They're doing just fine. Saul has it under control. He's winning the crowd over."

The next question came from a large man. "After such a long journey, what do you plan on doing now that you're in the City?"

"Another great question," Saul said. He suddenly felt a deep pain in his stomach, where his scar was. He pressed against it with his hand, and the pain slowly faded. "We plan on doing more things like this. Coming to events. Meeting people like you. Promoting the good work you do here in the Spire. Many people already know, but some don't. The Crowns attacked us the day we arrived because we showed support for Mr. Greene. If we can change their minds and stop their violence, the City will be a better place."

"What if you can't change their minds?"

"I believe almost anyone can be persuaded to the correct path, but if it comes down to it, we are willing to do whatever it takes. If that means taking on Simon's forces head on, then that's what we'll do. He can be a frightening man, but he doesn't scare us."

"He scares me," Ella said from backstage. "And we should be scared of him. He's killed countless numbers of innocent people without even batting an eye."

Rupert looked at her. "But that's not what the people need to hear right now. What they need is inspiration. Positive encouragement. They must believe that Vince and Saul can lead them to victory. That's the only way to get on Greene's good side."

"I know it's all an act," she said, "but he's so convincing."

"That's a good thing. That means he's doing his job."

Up next was a much smaller man. "Mr. Vigo sure is quiet up there. Does he have any words for us?"

Saul looked back. "Vince?"

Vince stepped forward. "I know I have not said much. I am a quiet person. Saul has done a wonderful job of expressing our enthusiasm for this partnership. We are excited for what's to come. We hope you are too." He stepped back to let Saul take over.

"There have never been truer words. Mr. Greene has shown us great hospitality. We look forward to working with him."

Greene stepped in front of him. "Well said. I am sorry to cut this short, but that will have to be the last question. I must speak with these two in private. There are many things to plan for the future. We hope you are as excited as we are."

The crowd stood up and clapped as Vince and Saul followed Greene offstage.

"You did a wonderful job up there," Ella said.

Greene patted them on the back. "They certainly did. The audience loves you."

"Why did you cut it short?"

"I received some news while we were up on stage. It is important that you know. Come with me. We'll go somewhere more private."

As they left the auditorium, the rumble of the crowd grew distant. Greene popped his head into an empty room and then waved for the others to come in. The room was nearly identical to the briefing room they were in before.

Alan sat down at the table and stretched out his legs. "What's so important?"

Greene paced around at the head of the table. "You may all want to sit for this." They all took a seat, leaning forward to hear the news. "We have the results from your scans. They came in while we were up on stage. All of you are completely healthy...except for Saul."

Saul looked up. "Why? What's wrong with me?"

"It is my understanding that you had an encounter with Barnabus Carbul. He shot you."

"Yeah, that's right." He rubbed the scar with his fingers. "But it's all healed up now. I'm fine."

"The wound has healed, but the bullet is still in there. Have you been feeling any pain?"

"I have, but I thought it was just part of the healing process."

Greene shook his head. "It isn't. That bullet is slowly killing you. If we don't get it out soon, you will die." They all went silent when they heard that last word. "I know that sounds scary, but you're in good hands. Our medical sector is the best in the City. I will personally make sure you get the best treatment. I have already scheduled an appointment with our most successful surgeon. He will see you in an hour" He walked to the door. "I have to tend to some business, but I will return when he's ready for you. Believe me when I say that I will do everything in my power to keep you alive. If you need anything at all while I'm gone, Charlotte can help you." He backed out of the door and left.

Saul slouched in his chair, staring down at the ground. The others gathered around him. "I can't die," he said. "What was the point in surviving the gunshot if I'm just going to die anyway?"

"You don't have to worry," Charlotte said. "There's no way he's going to let you die, especially after that conference. The people love you. You're supposed to be our success story. If you die, that all falls apart. Greene would never let that happen. I'm positive he's making your treatment his top priority."

"Then where did he go?" he asked. "Why did he leave instead of staying here with us?"

"You're his number one priority, but not his only priority. He still has to run the Spire and watch over the City. He's a very busy man."

"You can just drain something, right?" Alan asked. "It'll heal right up."

Vince shook his head. "Draining is what got him into this situation. The bullet is stuck in there. Draining isn't going to help."

"Stay optimistic," Ella said. "It sounds like they're well equipped to treat you."

"That's right," Charlotte said. "We have the best of the best in the Spire. It's one of the perks of working here. You work for Greene now. For all intents and purposes, you are all Spire employees. That means you get all of the benefits, including our state of the art healthcare."

"Does he pay us?" Alan asked.

"There's no need for money in the Spire. To compensate for the work we do, he provides food, housing, and entertainment. Ask for anything within the lines of reason and it's yours, as long as you keep up your work performance. If you're valuable to him, he'll take care of you. Right now Vince and Saul are extremely valuable."

"What happens if you underperform?"

"He fires you. He stops providing food and shelter, and he sends you back to the streets to take care of yourself. He takes his work very seriously, and if you aren't contributing, he's not afraid to get rid of you."

"That's harsh," Alan said. "But I guess that's how you get things done."

"Over the years, many people have come and gone. Those who stay longer earn Greene's trust. Many of us have been around for over a hundred years. Barnabus was over two hundred."

"Really?" Rupert said. "Greene doesn't seem too upset that we killed him."

"Barnabus was a loose cannon and Greene knew it. It was only a matter of time before something like that happened. Now that it has, he's moved on. Vince and Saul are the next big thing. You're far more valuable than Barnabus was. Of course, you wouldn't even be here if it wasn't for Barnabus. He was unconventional, but extremely loyal, a trait that Greene admires."

"How long have you worked here?" Alan asked.

"About fifty years in the Spire. Ten years as Vince and Saul's monitor agent."

"What were you doing for the other forty years?" Ella asked.

"I did a lot of small jobs. I was a soldier at one point. After that, I worked in the cosmetic sector, but that wasn't satisfying for me. I felt the urge to do more. So I worked my way up."

"And now you're a monitor agent," Rupert said.

"Yes. Being a monitor agent for such high profile subjects is a long-term job. It is extremely strenuous, twenty-four hours a day, seven days a week, but once it's all over, I'm done for good. Greene will continue to provide food and shelter for the rest of my life, and he'll slap a big paycheck in my hands. That's how all of the high profile monitor agent positions work. I have no family, and I can handle the stress, so this job is perfect for me."

"That's interesting and all," Saul said, "but I was just told I'm going to die. Can we focus on that?"

"That's what I'm saying," Charlotte said. "You're not going to die. Greene would never allow it."

SIXTEEN

G REENE LED THEM into the surgeon's office. A well-dressed man sat at his desk, flipping through documents. He wore a fitted black suit with the City logo patched on the shoulder.

"Welcome," he said, rising to his feet. He walked over and shook Greene's hand. "I take it these are our guests."

"That's right. These are the ones from outside."

"It must be fascinating out there."

"I wouldn't say fascinating," Rupert said. "It's…different."

"Fair enough. I'm Dr. Brant. It's a pleasure to meet all of you."

"He's the best we have in the Spire," Greene said. "Well-known for his many achievements."

"Thank you for the kind words," Dr. Brant said. He turned to Saul. "So this is my patient?"

Greene nodded. "Yes, it is. Please tell me you have good news."

"Let's all sit down and we can discuss the situation we have here." They all took a seat except for Greene, who stood near the back with his arms crossed. "I have been looking at your file for some time now. It is a very interesting case. I've never seen anything quite like it. I suppose it's because of your draining powers. You see, when the bullet entered your body, it punctured your lung. Without your powers, you would have died within a day. However, you manage to heal yourself and survive. Unfortunately, the rapid healing process managed to push the bullet in even further. It is now completely encased by your lung. You may have bought yourself some time, but it is slowly killing you."

"One of the Crown doctors looked at my wound," Saul said. "He said I'd be fine."

"I'm afraid the Crowns medical resources are nowhere near as sophisticated as ours. Our body scanners are top of the line."

"Is there a way to treat it?" Greene asked. "Can you remove the bullet?"

"Not without killing him. I'm afraid it's just too dangerous to operate. And draining will only worsen the situation." He paused. "I know it's hard to hear, but your days are limited. That bullet will slowly dig deeper into your lung and eventually it will kill you."

Saul's eyes filled with tears. "There has to be something you can do."

"The best I can do is inject you with one of the formulas we're testing. Theoretically, it should strengthen the tissue in your lung and slow the process. It's only a temporary solution, but it should buy you a month or two."

"You're absolutely sure you can't operate on him?" Greene asked.

"If I do, he will most likely die on the table."

"Very well." He looked to Saul. "I suggest you take that injection. It will give you time. Perhaps enough to bring Simon down."

The tears poured down Saul's face. He wiped the snot with the back of his hand. "That bastard is going down."

As the others gathered around to comfort him, Rupert approached Greene. "I have a quick question for you. Where is Fred, my falcon? They said they were fixing her up. Is she better yet?"

"They're still tending to her. Be patient. She'll be better in no time."

"I would like to check in on her. Can I see her?"

"I'm afraid we have a strict no-visitor policy in our medical sector. You will not be able to see her until she has fully healed."

"How long will that be? The nurse told me it would only be a day or two."

"It may be longer. We had to reconstruct part of her skeleton. The recovery time is quite long. But don't worry. She is in good hands."

Dr. Brant reached into a drawer and pulled out a syringe. "I have the injection right here. We can do it right now if you want. It's quick and painless."

Saul nodded. "Do it."

Dr. Brant stuck the needle in his arm and pushed the fluid in. "This will buy you some time. Use it wisely."

"We will make the most of his time," Greene said. He looked at Saul. "We'll take you around. You'll meet as many people as possible. Make the biggest impact that we can with the time you have left. You will make a difference. When your unfortunate end comes, people will know your name. You will be remembered as the hero of the City. The one who saved us all. The one who brought down Simon Hedcrown."

With those words, Saul looked back at Greene. *And I'm going to take you down too, son of a bitch.* He smiled. "Let's do it."

SEVENTEEN

THEY RETURNED TO the briefing room. The group, along with other Spire employees, filled the seats at the table. Greene stood at the front.

"One of our undercover agents has reported plans for a second attack." He pointed to the screen displaying a bird's eye view of the Spire and its defensive walls. "This is where Simon attacked last time." He pointed to the gap in the first wall. "It will likely be the target of his next attack. He is going to exploit that weakness while he still can. We're working on getting it repaired, but it will take some time. In the meantime, we need to protect that opening. We must guard it and make sure no one gets through. I have some men down there right now, but it's not enough. We need more. They certainly outnumber us, but we have the firepower to hold them off. Our new cannons worked perfectly last time. It scared them away. Next time, they'll know what they're up against. They'll be prepared for our cannons, so we need to increase our firepower. Move more of our cannons to that area. We have extra cannons on the third wall. I would like to move those up. That will scare them away."

One of the workers raised her hand. "That will leave the third wall vulnerable."

"That is true, but the chances of them making it that far are slim. Even if they do make it through that gap, the second wall is fully intact."

"Who else can we send down there?" she asked. Her hand was still raised. "Having more cannons means we need more people to operate them."

"As you all know, we have a shortage of troops at the moment. I sent a squad out to the streets to deal with an incident at one of our supply shops, but after Simon's last attack, I have called them back. They will arrive sometime tomorrow, but until then, we need volunteers. Anyone who wants to protect the Spire, now is a good time for patriotism. Volunteers will fight to protect what we've worked so hard to achieve." He looked to Vince and Saul. "That's where you two come in. A lot of these volunteers will be ordinary people, not soldiers. You need to inspire them. Remind them what they're fighting for."

"You want us to go down there with them?" Alan asked.

"Just these two. You three can do what you want. Go down with them or stay up here. It's up to you. But Vince and Saul need to be down there. Their presence will boost confidence and raise morale."

"What about me, sir?" Charlotte asked.

"You will go down as well. In the absence of a military commander, you will be in charge of our men. Put that military training of yours to use. You will also stay with Vince and Saul."

She nodded.

"The rest of you, go around and recruit any volunteers that are willing to fight for the Spire. If all goes according to plan, there will be no real danger. We just need numbers to keep them at bay. Once the wall is repaired, we will return to our normal procedures. Are there any questions?" There was no response. "Good. Then let's get to work."

Everyone dispersed from the table. Vince and the others gathered near the far side of the room.

"We're coming down with you," Alan said. "Wherever you go, we go."

"No," Vince said. "The three of you will stay up here."

"What? Why?"

"He's right," Rupert said. "This is the perfect time for us to look around and get familiar with the Spire without Charlotte watching our backs."

Ella looked up at the cameras. "She won't be watching, but someone will be."

"That is true," Vince said. "You will have to be very careful, but I believe it's possible to get around unseen. There must be blind spots. Walk around, act normal, and before you do anything suspicious, check for cameras. I want you to explore the area and find anything that may help us in the future. Our focus right now is Simon, but that doesn't mean we can't prepare for Greene. We should do our research, so when the time comes, we'll be ready."

"I agree," Rupert said.

"Saul and I will follow Greene's orders. We'll keep him happy. You explore as much as you can."

Charlotte, who had been speaking with Greene, finished up and walked over to the group. "When you're ready I can take you to the elevators. Will it be all of you?"

"No," Rupert said. "The three of us would like to get some rest. This whole process is very draining."

Charlotte nodded. "I understand. I'm quite tired myself, but I'll pull through." She turned to Vince and Saul. "Will you two be okay?"

"Yes," Vince said. "We don't need much sleep."

"Ah, that's right. I forgot that's one of the benefits of your formula." She turned back to the others. "If you change your mind, you can take the elevators at the end of the hall and meet us on level one. I can show you back to your rooms if you'd like."

Ella held up her hand. "That's not necessary. We remember the way."

"Very well. Vince, Saul, follow me." They left the briefing room and headed down the long corridor.

When they entered the elevator, Vince saw a panel of buttons. "Is the Spire really that tall?"

"That's right. A hundred and fifty stories. Impressive, huh?" She reached forward to press level one.

"Very impressive. It doesn't feel that tall from the inside."

She cracked a smile. "Just wait until you see it from the bottom."

"So what exactly does Greene want us to do down there?" Saul asked. "I know he wants us to inspire the people, but how do we do that?"

"Just be available to them. If they want to talk, talk with them. If they ask questions, answer them. It's as simple as that. They all know who you are. Just being around them will boost morale."

"Sounds easy enough," Vince said.

Saul looked at him. "It sounds too easy. Shouldn't we be doing something more important than just sitting around and waiting for Simon to attack us?"

"What do you suggest?" she asked.

"We should take the offensive. Attack him first."

"He has too many people. Far more than we have. It's easier to defend than it is to attack."

"Then how about a quieter approach? Have someone sneak in and kill him in his sleep."

"Greene is already doing that. We have several men undercover as we speak. But Simon is very careful about who he keeps nearby. Only his most trusted followers get to work closely with him."

"There has to be something we can do. You were in the surgeon's office. I'm dying. I don't have time to wait around for an attack."

"The fact is, Greene has thought this out very thoroughly. He has other plans for the future, but right now, we know there's an attack coming and where it will be. Those people out on the walls need your support, so that is your priority right now, not Simon. Once the wall is repaired, then we can start thinking up ways to take down Simon."

"She's right," Vince said. "This is our job right now. If Greene wants us to support the people, then that's what we'll do."

Saul grimaced. "Okay, but after this I'm going to speak with Greene and we're going to come up with a real plan.

"Very well," Charlotte said. "I'm sure he'll appreciate your input."

The elevator beeped and the doors opened up to a lobby area. "How are you doing?" said the secretary as they passed the front desk.

"We're wonderful," Charlotte said. "Thank you. How are you?"

"Same as usual. Are you going out to join them on the wall?"

"Yes, we are. Mr. Greene's orders. We have to prepare for Simon's next attack."

"It's scary, isn't it?"

"It is, but we'll be okay. We have Vince and Saul here to help us."

The secretary jumped from her seat. "Oh my god. It's Vince and Saul. I can't believe it. This is so exciting." She ran over and gave them a hug. "It's great that you support what we do. There are so many people who despise our work."

"Your work here is important," Saul said. "You improve people's lives. You *save* people's lives. You saved *our* lives."

"Yes, I heard about that. You've lived over two hundred years? That's crazy."

"Yes," Saul said. "Two hundred years. It's been quite a journey."

"And you've come all this way just to meet Mr. Greene. That's amazing."

"He is a great man. It was certainly worth the journey. The city is an amazing place."

"I've lived here my whole life. I can't imagine what it's like outside. I hear awful things."

Saul gave a strange look. "Awful? It's not awful. Just different."

"Sorry Judith," Charlotte said. "We're in a hurry. No time to chat."

"No worries. It was a pleasure meeting you two."

She waved, and they waved back.

"You see?" Charlotte said. "These people are curious about the outside world. They're excited to meet you and hear your stories. Just a simple conversation can lift their spirits."

They stepped outside, into the sunlight. Saul took a deep breath in. "Finally, some fresh air." In front of them stood the third wall. They walked across the grassy field towards the gate on the far side of the wall.

Before they reached it, Charlotte stopped. "Wait," she said. She turned around and pointed up. "Now isn't that a beauty?"

They turned around and looked up at the Spire, towering over them. It stuck up from the ground and pierced the sky. The sun glared off of the windows, creating a halo effect. "How high up were we?" Vince asked.

"We were near the top. Level one hundred and forty-nine, right under Greene. Like I said, the vitality sector is very important to him. He occupies the top floor, and can visit the vitality labs whenever he wants."

"I have to admit," Saul said, "it is beautiful."

Vince gazed up with him. "It sure is."

"It takes my breath away every time," Charlotte said. She looked up one more time and then continued walking. "As much as I would like to stay here, people are waiting for us on the first wall."

EIGHTEEN

ELLA, ALAN, AND Rupert returned to their bedroom after parting with Vince and Saul. They sat on their beds and rested their feet. Ella stood up. "Are you ready? Let's do some exploring."

"Where should we start?" Alan asked.

"Let's go back to the medical sector," Rupert said. "I want to find Fred."

"They said they're working on her, right?"

"They did. I just want to check in on her. Greene said they have a strict no-visitor policy, but it doesn't hurt to try."

"I agree," Ella said. "We should find Fred to make sure she's okay. She's with strangers, and she's far from home. She might be scared."

Alan nodded. "Sounds like a plan." He walked out the door and glanced down the hall in both directions. "Do either of you remember the way?"

"Not exactly," Ella said, "but it's on this floor. I know that."

"That doesn't help much. These floors are humungous. I don't know how anyone finds anything around here."

Rupert pointed down the hall. "There's a map on the wall over there."

They walked over and examined the map. It had a large display of lines twisting and turning and crossing each other. They tilted their head to get a different perspective.

"There's no structure to it at all," Alan said. "It's just chaos. There are so many hallways with no pattern. How are we going to find the medical sector with this?"

Rupert picked a direction and started walking. "I guess we'll just have to wander around. We're bound to find it eventually."

"There has to be a better way," Alan said as he trotted to catch up with him. "It could take ages."

"Asking someone is not going to help. They're not going to tell us how to get into a restricted area."

"Hey," Ella called from behind them. "I think it's this way. I remember this hallway."

"They all look the same," Alan said. "It's impossible to tell where we've been and where we haven't."

She pointed. "That's the monitor room Charlotte showed us. It's this way. I'm positive."

Alan shrugged. "As long as one of us knows where we're going."

"I really think I do." She looked at another map on the wall. "Yes, we go down this hallway and take a left. Then all we have to do is go straight until we hit the medical sector."

"If you say so."

"Ella has always had a good sense of direction," Rupert said. "If anyone can navigate this maze, it's her."

"I don't doubt her. I'm just getting frustrated. These last few days have been long."

"They certainly have," Rupert said. "Hopefully, we can fit in some time to rest."

Ella looked back. "I get a feeling we won't have much time to rest."

"Vince and Saul certainly won't," Alan said. "Those two are superstars around here. Greene has a lot of plans for them."

"I feel bad for Saul," Ella said. "Of all the people that deserve to die, he's not one of them."

"Simon and Greene," Rupert said, "they're both very different people, but I would fit both of them into that category. People that deserve to die."

"Saul is a good guy. It's no wonder Vince gets along with him."

"They've been best friends since they were kids. Nothing can break that bond. Not even two hundred years of separation. I can tell Vince really cares about him."

"Everyone they've known has passed away. They've only got each other. I can't even imagine what that's like."

"They have us too," Alan said.

"But eventually, we'll just be memories to them. Friends from the past as they move on to something else."

"You make it sound like living forever is a bad thing."

"Do you think it's a good thing?" Rupert asked. "Could you really stand living forever with things constantly changing around you? The people, the places, everything you know just fading away. It would be a lonely life."

"But they don't *have* to live forever."

"If you were given that power, even if you wanted to stop, could you? All of us are afraid of death, but we don't have a choice."

"They have more of that formula around here somewhere. You could probably get your hands on some."

"I wouldn't want it. That power would haunt me for the rest of my days."

Alan thought about it. "Yeah, I guess you're right. I wouldn't want it either."

"They didn't know what they were getting into when they first met Barnabus," Ella said. "If they did, they never would have followed him back into the woods."

"It must have been tempting," Alan said. "The promise of immortality. Especially at such a young age. I wouldn't take it now, but thirty years ago, I wouldn't even think twice." As they walked through the corridor, they saw a sign hanging from the ceiling. *Medical Sector.* "Ella was right. I had faith in her the whole time."

"Sure you did," Ella said snidely.

They walked past the sign and entered the waiting room. There were no patients waiting. No people at all. They wandered through the rows of chairs, towards the door on the other side.

As they got closer, the door swung open, and a nurse walked into the room. "Hello there. Ella. Rupert. Alan."

She nodded her head with each name. "How may I help you?"

"We wanted to check in on Fred," Rupert said. "How is she doing?"

"I'm afraid we can't let you see her while she is still in recovery, but I assure you she is just fine. She is safe and sound in our blue room."

"When will I be able to see her?"

"It's hard to say. The recovery time varies depending on the circumstances. You will certainly see her within a month."

"A month?" Alan asked. "Really? That long?"

"Again, it varies, but we have had subjects go up to a month in recovery."

Rupert nodded. "Is there a way I can check her status? I would like to stay informed."

"Come back here whenever you want. I'll be more than happy to give you an update."

"Very good. Thank you for your help."

"My pleasure." She stepped back and closed the door behind her.

"What do you think?" Alan asked. He held a skeptical look on his face.

Rupert looked up at the cameras. They were posted in each corner of the room. "I think we need to sneak in."

"My thoughts exactly," Ella said as she studied the cameras as well. "Do you see any blind spots?"

"I don't. Not anywhere useful."

Alan pushed on the door. "It's open. What if we just go in?" When he pushed it again, the nurse pulled it open.

"I'm sorry, but this area is restricted. Employees and patients only. If you need any assistance, I can help you, or you can call any of our nurses on the computer over there. If they're on shift, they will be right out to assist you. Currently, I am the only nurse working in this sector right now, but I would be happy to help."

"We're okay for now," Rupert said. "We'll let you know if we need anything. Thank you." The nurse shut the door again. Rupert walked toward the exit of the room and signaled for them to follow. "If she's the only one on shift right now, you two can distract her, and I can sneak in."

Alan chuckled. "I like your thinking."

"Someone else will notice, right?" Ella asked. "There must be other people watching through the cameras?"

"It doesn't hurt to try," Rupert said. "Worst case, they tell us to leave. I'll say I got lost. I should have at least a few minutes to look around before anyone comes to kick me out."

"That sounds like a solid plan to me," Alan said.

Ella nodded. "Right. Alan and I will distract her. You go find Fred. The nurse said the blue room. Hopefully, Fred's okay. She's been by herself for a long time."

"She's a strong bird," Rupert said, "but I am getting a little worried."

Alan patted his back. "Don't worry. You'll find her. I'm sure she's fine. You wait here for your cue." They broke up, and Ella and Alan turned the corner. Alan knocked on the door and waited.

After a minute, the nurse returned, with a wide smile stretched across her face. "Hello." She glanced around the empty waiting room. "What happened to Rupert?"

"He was feeling a bit tired," Ella said. "He went back to the room to lie down."

"That's a good idea. You all must be very tired."

"We sure are," Alan said, "but it's tough to get any rest around here with all of the stuff that's been going on."

"Yes, it is for us too. All of the other nurses are down on the wall. They need to be ready for Simon's attack. They left me in charge up here. Though there isn't much to be in charge of. I've just been sitting around."

"So that's why there's no one around," Ella said. "We've been trying to find someone to give us a tour, but the place is a ghost town. We've been here a whole day and have barely seen anything."

"I suppose I could show you around."

"Really? If you don't mind, that would be lovely."

"Sure, why not? Nothing's going to happen while I'm gone. I'll give you a quick tour of this level. It should only be ten or fifteen minutes." She walked past them towards the main hallway. "Follow me."

She turned the corner as Rupert backed into the shadows. The three of them passed by and headed down the hall. Rupert slipped around the corner. He stared at the cameras as he dashed across the room, towards the door on the opposite side. He pushed the door open to a long empty hallway.

He made his way through, pushing open each door and sticking his head in. The rooms were color coded. Red. Green. White. Pink. And they were all empty. The last room on the right held a monitor showing footage from the waiting room, as well as other parts of the medical sector. When he reached the end, the corridor split in two. He looked left, then right. Both paths were identical. He turned right and continued walking. Orange. Silver. Purple. Blue. The nurse had said the *blue room*. He stopped and pushed the blue door open.

The room was similar to the one he woke up in when he first arrived in the Spire. There was a bed next to the large window overlooking the vast view of the City. Near the bed were various machines stacked on top of each other. The day he arrived, they were beeping like crazy, but today they were silent.

There was no Fred.

He opened all of the drawers and cabinets. Flipped through papers and files for any sign of her. Maybe they left her file out. Maybe they transferred her to another room. Maybe the nurse was mistaken, and Fred was in a different room completely. He looked up, saw a camera staring right at him, and looked back down to ruffle through more papers.

When he found nothing, he sat down on the bed, not sure what to do next. He glanced at the camera again. He was running out of time. Someone had surely noticed he was in a restricted area by now. If he was going to do something, he had to do it fast. He got up and left the blue room, continuing down the hall and examining each color as he passed. Maybe there was more than one blue room. Black. Gold. Yellow. Gray. Brown. He reached a dead end. He turned around and ran back to where the hallway split. Maroon. Peach. Beige. Cyan. Maybe cyan was blue? He opened the cyan door and found it in the same condition as the blue room. Empty and useless.

He turned around and bumped into Greene, standing firmly at the entrance of the room. His feet were shoulder width apart, and his hands were interlocked behind his back. "You have gotten a bit lost, haven't you?"

Rupert remained calm. "Yes, it appears so. It's so easy to get lost around here. I'm afraid I have no idea where I am. I was trying to get back to my room. I'm quite tired and wanted to rest."

A huge smile was plastered across Greene's face. "No worries. I can personally escort you right back to your room."

Rupert followed him down the hall. "Thank you. That would be very helpful. I know you're a busy man. It's so nice of you to help me in person."

"It's my pleasure. I try to connect with people whenever I can. Unfortunately, I spend way too much time up on the top floor. There are too many things that require my attention, but every once in a while I get to help someone out like this."

Rupert peeked into the room with the monitor as they passed by. The screen followed them as they walked, with the words, *Restricted Personnel*, blinking in red letters.

Greene still held his friendly smile as he spoke. "It's always nice to help the people. They need my leadership. They need better technology. That's why I do tests."

Rupert nodded. "The tests have brought you far. You have technology that baffles me. Things that I never would have imagined. It is very impressive. The Spire alone is an engineering marvel."

They passed through the waiting room and into the main corridor.

"It took a long time to build what we have, but I am damn proud of what we've accomplished. And I don't plan on stopping. We're going full speed ahead. Building. Discovering. Achieving."

"What kind of things are you researching right now?"

"There are many things. We just finished our latest model of the cannon, which proved to be a huge success during Simon's attack. Our transportation sector is looking at flight right now. They are trying to find ways to mimic a bird's wings. They've come very close to independent flight, but there is still some work to be done. Once they hit their breakthrough, it will be huge for the Spire." They turned a corner. "And then, of course, there's our vitality tests, which your friends are a part of. We've been working on this one for a long time. Vince and Saul received an early formula that has gone through many iterations since then. I'm trying to achieve a vitality formula that doesn't require draining on a regular basis. Draining is unsustainable and impractical, something your friends have probably learned." They stopped in front of the door to his room. "Here we are. If you ever get lost again, feel free to wave down one of these cameras. Someone will see."

"Thank you. I hope to learn my way around soon enough."

Greene nodded and continued down the hall. Rupert entered the room and sat down on his bed, thinking about what had happened. Fred was not in the medical sector. Greene clearly did not want him to know that. So where was she? Why did they lie to him? What were they hiding?

NINETEEN

VINCE AND SAUL stood atop the front wall, peering down at the damage Simon had done. Most of the debris near the gap was cleared out. Workers were dragging away remaining bits of rubble to make room for the new construction. Scaffolding already surrounded the opening as they moved materials from the bottom of the wall to the top.

Charlotte stood beside them, watching as well. "It's amazing how fast they work, huh?"

Vince nodded. "At this rate, they'll be done by tomorrow. Maybe sooner. Just look at them go. Simon needs to act fast if he wants to exploit this weak spot."

"I wouldn't call it a weak spot," Saul said. "There are so many people here, and so many cannons, it's probably the strongest part of the wall right now."

"That's the point," Charlotte said. "Turn your weakness into your strength. A rule to live by. That's something Greene understands very well and uses often."

"What are Greene's weaknesses?" Saul asked. "He seems like a man with no kinks in his armor."

"Exactly," Charlotte said.

"He must have something. Everyone has something."

"If he does, he hides it well." She stared off at the buildings in the distance. "Simon and Greene are both powerful men, but Simon has many flaws. Greene elevates himself and feeds off the people's energy. Simon takes that energy and turns it into fear. Say what you will about Greene, but he is a respectable man. Simon's a savage."

"How has Simon stayed in power for so long?" Vince asked. "Greene must have the resources to stop him."

"Simon's forces grow every day. People are afraid of him. He's a loose cannon, and they're scared to fight against him, so they join him instead. The Crowns are growing fast, and Greene is just barely keeping up. That's why we need the two of you to help rally the people and crush the fear that he spreads."

"Were the Crowns always like that? Were they always so violent?"

"That's how it was with Simon's father. Harry was the only respectable Hedcrown. He built the Crowns on good intentions and genuine principles. When Robert took over, the Crowns took a turn for the worst. They grew more violent and radical. They started hurting innocent people in order to gain the advantage. And when Simon took over, things only got worse. The Crowns broke down into organized chaos. Wherever they go, they leave a path of destruction. They're guided by Harry's principles, but they've twisted them into a false sense of justice. The worst part is, they make some good points. Some of the things Simon talks about makes sense, but when you dig deeper, all you find is destruction fueled by anger and fear."

"But you've seen what Greene puts people through," Vince said. "What he's put us through. How can you support that?"

She turned around to gaze at the Spire. "I may not agree with him all the time, but given the choice between Greene and Simon, I would choose Greene. Every time."

"Why do you have to choose?" Saul asked. "I've already made my choice. It's neither of them."

"I know you don't take kindly to Greene, but the truth is, without him the City would break down. He keeps everything in order. We need someone like that to survive as a society."

"Then find someone else. Find someone that you're proud to support. You shouldn't have to settle for Greene because he's the one in charge right now. You can change that and make the City a better place for everyone."

"How do we find someone like that?"

"I don't know, but there must be someone that can do the job better than Greene."

Charlotte looked down to the ground, shaking her head. "I don't think we could survive without him."

"That's what he wants you to think, but the reality is, he's just as expendable as anyone else. You think the City will go bonkers without him. There's only one way to find out. Once we're done dealing with Simon, Greene's next."

Vince looked over. "Saul, don't."

"What? She already knows that's why we're here. You're insulting her intelligence by suggesting otherwise."

"It's true," Charlotte said. "I know you're here to kill Greene, but I'm the only one that knows. It's important that we keep it that way. We can't have the heroes of the Spire openly speaking treason."

"Don't worry," Vince said. "We plan on fully cooperating. Right, Saul?"

"Right. As much as I hate Greene, you're right. Simon is much worse. If we have to work with Greene to take down that monster, then so be it."

"I'm glad," Charlotte said. She looked around at the people, who were starting to gather around them. "I've scheduled a meetup session while we wait. You're going to meet the people. Don't be shy. They're all very excited to see you. Are you ready?"

They nodded.

At the wave of her hand, the crowd gathered in and swarmed around them. They all held pens and various items to sign. Vince and Saul were overwhelmed. So much of their lives were spent in solitude, and now mobs of people wanted to see them and talk to them. They signed what they could, but when a loud horn echoed from behind, the people scattered.

Charlotte waved them by as they passed. "Come on, let's go! You know what the horn means. Get back to your posts!"

Vince looked to Charlotte, puzzled. "What's going on?"

"We have sensors along the perimeter of Spire territory. That was the first warning horn. It sounds when someone crosses one of them. This could be Simon. The second horn indicates friend or foe. It's a long tone if they're friendly, and a short burst if they aren't."

They waited for the next horn. Vince gazed at the empty streets in front of them. There was nothing. No movement at all. Completely vacant. "How long does the second horn usually take?"

Charlotte looked around at the others. "Usually not this long. Something's wrong."

At that moment, five short bursts rang over the speakers, this time, lower in tone.

"Crap!" Charlotte said.

The people beside them dashed off to the right.

"What's going on now?" Saul asked. "What do five bursts mean?"

"It means we're in the wrong spot. This is Post One along the wall. They're coming from Post Five. That's on the opposite end. We have to get over there fast." She saw more men and women running off. "No!" she yelled. "Not everyone goes. Some of you stay here and watch the gap. We can't let anyone sneak by." She turned to Vince and Saul. "You two come with me. We're going to Post Five." She sprinted along the wall, and Vince and Saul followed.

"How long is this wall?" Vince yelled.

"It's long. That's why we're in such a rush. The horns give us a few minutes of warning, but we don't have much time."

"What if they attack the gap, too?"

"There was no Post One horn, so we should be okay. If they do attack Post One, the horn will give us some time to shift some troops back. Right now, Simon's main force is at the other end of this wall."

"Damn, that son of a bitch is crafty," Saul said as they sprinted down the narrow path.

Charlotte looked to one of the troops running beside her. "Do we have the cannons set up over there?"

"No ma'am. They are at Post Four."

"Damn! Roll them down to Post Five and prepare to fire. We have no time to waste."

"Yes ma'am!" he yelled, and dashed ahead.

"This is going to get interesting," she said.

"How long do the cannons take to set up?" Vince asked.

"A long time. They're new and very powerful, but they're loading process is slow. Greene is putting more into production, but until then, there is a bit of a shortage. We have to pick and choose where to deploy them. Obviously, Post One is a priority, so most of our cannons are there, but we have a few extras at Post Four. Lucky for us, they're not at Post Two. There's no way we would've moved them in time."

"Do we have anything other than cannons?" Saul asked.

"Of course. We have guns, but they're not as threatening. We developed the cannons to match the impact of Simon's bombs."

"But we can defend without them," Vince said.

"Yes, but it will be harder. I can't imagine this attack will be bigger than the last, but you never know. He might have some tricks up his sleeves. He is, as you put it, a crafty son of a bitch."

They passed a sign displaying a large number two. Vince saw it as they dashed past. "One down, three to go."

Charlotte looked back at him. "Hope you don't tire easily."

"Don't worry about us," Saul said. "We've got this vitality stuff, remember? Just make sure to keep up." He dashed up next to her and took the lead.

Vince smiled. "That's the competitive Saul I remember." He passed Charlotte as well, and pulled up next to Saul.

Saul turned his head. "Oh, so it's like old times, huh?"

Vince nodded. "Like old times." He flashed a smile and took the lead. Saul kept right on his tail.

TWENTY

AFTER THE LONG run, Vince and Saul reached the end of the wall, Post Five. They both hunched over to catch their breath.

"You've still got it," Saul said. "You've always been number one."

"With admirable competition. It was a very close second." He looked back behind. "We must have lost Charlotte."

"I guess so." Saul looked over his shoulder to make sure no one was around. "Honestly, what do you think of her? Can we trust her?"

"She works for Greene. I don't know if we can trust any of these people."

"But the way she talks about him…she's different. When the time comes, I think we could get her to help us take down Greene."

"Weren't you listening?" Vince asked, shaking his head. "She works for him. Why would she help us?"

"She only works for him because she believes he's the better choice, which is true, but once Simon is gone, that choice is gone too."

"She does seem unsure about him. Do you really think she would turn on him?"

Saul nodded. "I do. If we can convince her, she will be very useful. She knows her way around the Spire and has access to places we don't. And most importantly, Greene trusts her. She can get close to him."

"We *might* be able to turn her against Greene. *Maybe* free some test subjects. But there's no way you could get her to *kill* Greene."

"I'm not saying she has to kill him, but she could spy on him. Sabotage his plans."

"And how do we convince her?"

"I haven't thought that far ahead yet. Either way, now isn't the time to think about it. Let's focus on Simon. Once he's gone, we can plan our next moves."

Charlotte trotted up behind them. "You two are fast," she said as she panted. "Did I miss anything? Has he come yet?"

"Not yet," Vince said. "We still have time to set up the cannons."

"Great, come help me with this one. They're too heavy for one person to move."

They crouched next to the cannon and pushed all at once. It moved only a few feet. "Christ! Why are these so heavy?" Saul asked.

"It's solid metal. It's designed that way. Otherwise, when we fire, the thing would go flying off the wall. That's what happened with some of the earlier models."

They pushed again and almost made it to the front barrier. "One more push should do it," She said as she leaned into the metal and pushed off of the ground. The wheels locked into place. "Good, now let's get it loaded."

Vince studied at the metal behemoth. "How do we do that?"

She pointed to a brick sized cylinder at Saul's feet. "Grab one of those and slide it in."

Saul bent down to pick it up. "What's in this?"

"That is full of black powder."

"Black powder?" he repeated as he pushed it through the opening at the front of the barrel.

"It's explosive." She came around holding a large rod. "It's similar to the stuff Simon uses to make his bombs." She slid the rod into the hole and pushed the black powder further down. She pointed next to the cylinders. "Now hand me one of those cannonballs."

Saul bent down again and grabbed one with both hands. "Wow, this thing is heavy."

"That's why it's so effective. In a crowd of people, it can take out a good dozen in one shot."

He handed it over to her. "Holy crap. I'm a little afraid to use this thing now."

She dropped the cannonball in the hole and pushed it down. "It's not something to mess around with if you don't know what you're doing."

"Great," Saul said. "*We* don't know what we're doing."

"But *I* do. I'm trained. Just let me operate the cannon. That's not your job. Your job is to boost morale. Keep these people's spirits up. It's a little chaotic right now, but I'm sure they could use a few words of inspiration."

Vince looked at Saul, who nodded. "Yeah, yeah, I got this."

"You're better at speaking than I am."

Saul stepped in front of the people, who were running back and forth with bricks of black powder and cannonballs in their hands. He stuck two fingers in his mouth and blew with force. A loud whistle echoed along the wall. The people stopped where they were, and looked up at Saul.

"Everyone! Simon may have caught us off guard, and we may be a mess right now, but what I've seen come out of this is the shining example of why you are all so great. You have come together and conquered chaos. I haven't been in the City long, but one thing I've learned is that Simon must be stopped. He is a mad man. Unpredictable. A danger to every single person in the City. Some of you may be scared as you set up those cannons, but your bravery is not only a service to Victor Greene or the Spire. It is a service to the City as a whole. Don't let Simon take what isn't his. Don't let him spread his chaos even further. Conquer the chaos like you have done today and crush it into the ground. He thinks he can outsmart us, but he has no idea who he's dealing with. Let's show him!"

People clapped and cheered. Saul smiled and turned back to Charlotte, who finished loading the cannon.

"Good work," she said. "Short, but sweet. It got the job done." She looked off at the buildings. "Now we just wait for the Crowns."

Vince and Saul leaned against the front barrier, scanning the landscape for movement. There was nothing. Just the gentle breeze of a mild afternoon. Vince looked back. "How far are the sensors? Should it take this long?"

"It usually isn't this long, but it has happened before."

Another low horn blared from the speakers. This time just one.

"They're back at Post One," Saul said.

"It's okay." Charlotte kept her eyes fixed straight ahead. "We still have people posted there. It looks like they're splitting in two."

The sound of hollers and cheers played through the speakers. Saul flinched, startled by the volume. "What is that?"

"Artificial battle noise," Charlotte said. "It gives the illusion of a massive army behind these walls. It's one of Greene's defense tactics."

"He's a smart guy."

She nodded. "He's always thinking of new ways to outsmart Simon."

There was movement in the distance. They leaned forward to see what it was. There was a child, a little boy no more than eight years old, walking towards them.

"Hold your fire," Charlotte commanded.

The boy continued walking. Another appeared behind him. And then another. Soon there were several dozens, both boys and girls, approaching the wall.

"What do we do?" Charlotte said.

"Well, we're not about to shoot a bunch of kids," Saul said, "right?"

"Hold on," she said as she pressed her finger to her ear. A look of regret stretched across her face. She lifted her arm above her head. "Prepare to fire!"

"What?" Saul shouted.

"Those are Greene's orders."

"We can't kill a bunch of kids. Vince, we can't let this happen."

Vince shook his head. "I agreed to follow Greene's orders, but Saul is right. This is too much."

"The orders come directly from Greene. We must follow them. He knows what he's doing."

"He knows he's about to kill dozens of innocent kids," Saul said. "You and him both know that's not right."

"What I know, is that when we ignore orders, it invites chaos. In a time of battle, we need order. If he says fire, we fire."

"So you just follow him blindly? That's exactly what those kids are doing down there. They're following orders without thinking clearly. Everyone around here is insane."

She lit a torch and held it over the wick. "Ready!"

"Wait!" Saul yelled. "Just listen to me!"

"Aim!"

"Don't ignore me! Vince, do something!" Vince shrugged, not sure what to do.

Charlotte looked at them and whispered, "Sorry guys." The flame from her torch tickled the end of the wick. "Fire—"

Saul charged into her with his full weight. She bumped into the side of the cannon, nudging its aim to the left, and dropped her torch. The flame bounced off the metal casing and landed directly on the wick. A single burst shot from the barrel and the cannonball launched into the distance. It veered off to the left and hit nothing but dirt.

The others held their torches still, but did not fire. Instead, they stared at Saul, who lay on the ground next to Charlotte. Vince ran over to help him up.

Saul stood before the others and projected his voice. "What we do up here on this wall is important. And it is important that we do the *right* thing. Greene may want you to kill these children, but they're misguided. They're not evil or dangerous—"

A loud pop rumbled the wall. The ground shook beneath their feet as the smell of gunpowder rose from below.

"Bombs!" Charlotte yelled. "They have bombs strapped to them! Shoot them down before they can get to the wall!"

The children charged ahead, screaming at the top of their lungs. The cannonballs flew from the wall and tore through mobs of younglings. Patches of explosions sprinkled the battlefield as bombs ignited. More groups of children emerged from the buildings, running full force towards the Spire.

"There are too many," Charlotte said. "They're getting through."

A small cluster reached the base of the wall and set off their charges. The wall rumbled again, this time more violently. Another explosion hit, and a crack ran up and over the wall.

"It's not going to hold!" She screamed to the others. "Move out of the way!"

They scattered away from the crack, pushing the cannons along with them. Vince looked down and watched another cluster hit the wall. And then another. The crack grew with each hit, until finally, it crumbled. Chunks of wall toppled over, crushing the bodies below and setting off more explosions. Debris shot up in every direction as the children climbed over the rubble and into the newly formed gap in the wall. They poured through and ran towards the second wall.

"They've broken through! Don't let them reach the second wall!"

But it was too late. They bombarded the second wall with a barrage of explosions.

"What do we do?" Vince asked. "We have nothing over there. All of our firepower is here."

She turned to everyone else, on both sides of the gap. "There's nothing we can do about those who get through. Focus your fire on the choke point." She pointed down at the bottleneck forming around the small opening. "Let's just hope the second wall can take a few hits."

They aimed their cannons downward and fired at the ground. Chunks of guts and debris flew into the air. Blood sprayed across the wall in a fine mist. Bodies piled up around the gap until there were no more. The last few explosions went off behind them, hitting the second wall and forming a crack. They turned around to see the final boy hurl himself into the stone. Flames engulfed him as he burst into a glorious ball of fire. The crack opened up and the stone crumbled in on itself. The second wall had fallen.

"Crap!" Charlotte said. "Greene isn't going to like that."

Vince and Saul looked down at the mess that was plastered about the ground. Mangled flesh and bones, twisting intestines, bloodied brains. They stared in awe at the aftermath of a ruthless massacre.

Saul lowered his head. "What have we done?"

"We did what we had to do," Charlotte said, placing a hand on his shoulder.

He shook it off. "No." His head jolted up, and he glared at her with piercing eyes. "No! This is not right. We're not the good guys. We can't be. Not after that."

Vince remained standing at the edge, staring down.

"Calm down," Charlotte said.

"Calm down?" His eyes darted back and forth. "Calm down? How can I be calm when we just murdered dozens of children? How are all of you okay with this?"

"We were following orders," she answered. "It was Greene's decision, not ours."

"Screw Greene. He doesn't own me. I don't have to follow his orders." He shook his head in frustration. "You don't just follow orders blindly. You think first. You have to think for yourself, and maybe recognize that what you just did is not okay."

Vince finally pulled his view from the horrifying scene and turned around. He grabbed Saul's arm. "Come on, let's go."

Saul resisted. "I'm not going any—"

Vince glared into his eyes with intense urgency and raised his voice. "I said, let's go."

They turned and marched back towards Post One. Charlotte followed.

TWENTY-ONE

VINCE AND SAUL pushed through the front doors to find Greene, waiting for them in the lobby. He stared at them with piercing eyes. "Come with me," he said, walking to the elevator. Charlotte jogged up behind. He held up his hand and shook his head. "You wait here. We'll be back."

The three of them entered the elevator, waiting in silence. Vince stole a glance at Greene. His face was stone and his eyes held purpose. When the doors opened, they followed him out. His pace was fast, but calm.

They followed him into a monitor room. Greene flipped the lights on, shut the door, and glared at Saul. "What the hell was that?" His tone was direct.

Saul flinched at his sudden change. "That was me disobeying an order."

"We had a deal. You cooperate and help me get Simon."

"I never agreed to murder a bunch of kids."

"They were going to die anyway!" he said. His voice was just below a shout. "They had bombs strapped to their chests. They damaged our second wall because of you. You disobeyed a direct order in front of my people. You cannot do that. I will not let it happen again."

"I'm not going to blindly follow your orders. I don't care what our deal was."

"If that's the case, maybe I should kill you."

Vince and Saul exchanged a nervous look.

"I know you're here to kill me, so why would I keep you around if you're not going to play by my rules?"

"You can't kill us," Vince said. "The people look up to us. They think we're heroes. We have just as much power as you do. You saw how they acted around Saul down there. They treated him like you, like their leader."

Greene grinned. "Everything you say is true. The people *do* look up to you. They would certainly be upset if you died. It looks like I've dug myself a hole, haven't I? But that's why I have insurance." He flipped a switch to turn on the monitors.

Vince looked up at the glowing screens. What he saw made his stomach turn. It was Snow Peak. Troops marched along the road. People lined up in a row, on their knees, with their hands tied behind their backs. He saw Ella's mom, Alan's wife, Martha, Horace, and even Carl. "You can't."

"I have no choice. You've forced my hand. I was going to give you a chance. I knew you were here to kill me, but I thought I could change your mind. Maybe you would finally understand what I'm trying to achieve with the tests. I'm only trying to help. I was hoping you would see that I'm not such a bad guy after all." He looked to Saul. "But your little outburst makes it abundantly clear that that will never happen." He tapped the glass monitor with his finger. "I can't kill *you*, but I *can* kill them. I know you two don't have too many people you care about, at least, not anymore." He pointed to Vince. "But you seem to be quite fond of your little group from Snow Peak. I think Saul's starting to warm up to them too. So I've taken their loved ones as collateral."

"You're sick," Saul said with disgust.

"That may be true. I suppose it doesn't matter. Either way, you'll cooperate. If you don't, every single one of them dies. If you disobey me, they're dead. If you resist me in any way, they're dead. And if you decide to kill me, if I can't check in with my troops each morning, all of your friends are dead. Do you understand me?"

They both stared with disbelief and lowered their heads. "So what now?" Vince asked.

"We continue as planned. Nothing changes. You will rally the people and help us fight Simon."

"And after that?"

"After that, I will let you free. You will leave the City and never come back."

"What about our friends?"

"The same goes for them. I will pull my troops from Snow Peak and they will all be safe and sound."

"I guess we have no option," Vince said. He looked sternly at Saul. "We will cooperate, right Saul?"

Saul answered with a look of disdain. He wanted to scream, to tell Greene he was crazy, but he knew he couldn't. He had never been to Snow Peak, had never met these people, but he saw Vince cared about them, and that was enough to keep him restrained. "Right, we will do what you say. We will follow your orders."

"Good." He leaned in and held a sharp glare. "I'm not messing around. One mistake and people die. Do you understand?"

They nodded.

A grin stretched back across Greene's face. "I knew you would. You are both very smart. That's why we chose you as subjects in the first place."

He checked the time on his watch. "Return to your rooms. I'll send for Charlotte and tell her to meet you there. We will have another meeting. The second wall has fallen. That has never happened before. The people will want to hear me speak." He looked at Saul. "No more outbursts. That will only confuse them. From now on, the only words that leave your mouth are in my favor. Simon is quick. We must plan our next move now soon." He opened the door and let them out. "Expect to hear from me in an hour."

As they walked down the hall to their room, Vince turned to Saul. "I think it's best we don't tell the others."

"Why? They should know. It's their home that's at stake."

"We need them to be sharp. Knowing that Greene is holding Snow Peak hostage will bring out strong emotions. It will cloud their judgment."

"And you still plan on killing Greene."

Vince nodded. "They won't agree if they know what's at stake."

"With good reason. How are you going to kill Greene without killing everyone in Snow Peak? You heard what he said. If his troops don't hear back from him, their orders are to kill."

"I don't know how," Vince said, "but we'll do it."

TWENTY-TWO

WHEN THEY GOT back to the room, Rupert, Alan, and Ella were sitting on their beds. "How did it go on the wall?" Ella asked. "We could see the explosions from up here. We were worried."

"They broke through the second wall," Vince said.

"What?" Alan asked, surprised. "How? Those walls are massive."

"That crazy bastard used kids. He strapped bombs to them and sent them to their death," Saul said.

Alan stood from his bed. "Jeez, this guy is nuts."

Ella covered her mouth. "Oh my god," she said. "Well, that's why we agreed to stop him, right? Crazy people are dangerous with that kind of power."

"He didn't earn the power either," Rupert said. "The only reason he's in charge is because he's got Hedcrown blood in him. This rebellion needs to happen, but he shouldn't be the one leading it."

"Unfortunately, he is," Vince said. "If he's willing to use kids as bombers, there's no telling what he'll do next."

"Right, the next thing you know we'll be fighting off puppies."

"This is no time to joke, Alan." Vince walked over and stood beside them. "A lot of children died today."

Alan lowered his head in respect. "You're right. I apologize."

"How did things go up here?" Saul asked.

"Not too well," Rupert said. "I managed to sneak into the medical sector, but I didn't find anything. Fred wasn't there. I don't know where she is. I think their hiding something. If they're lying about Fred, who knows what else they've been lying about."

Alan put a hand on his shoulder. "Don't worry buddy. We'll find Fred. She's tough as nails, that bird."

Rupert nodded.

"So what next? Greene must be uneasy with the second wall down. He might even be distracted enough for us to turn on him. Take him down while he's busy fighting Simon."

"No," Vince said. "We must stick to the plan. Focus on Simon first. Once he's taken care of, we can turn our attention to Greene. They both need to go, there's no question about that. But we need Greene's resources to deal with Simon. Once Greene trusts us, we can stab him in the back."

Saul snickered to himself. Greene would never trust them, but he played along anyway. "That's right, he has already given us more responsibilities. With a little more time, he'll accept us as his own."

"Tomorrow, Greene's troops arrive," Vince said. "The people we met on the wall today were not dangerous. They will not be a problem when we make our move. It's his troops I'm worried about. They're trained. When they arrive, I will observe them to see how they behave. I will gauge their level of training. We need to know how much trouble they'll give us."

Rupert nodded. "So you'll be down there with the troops. We'll stay up here and keep looking around."

"Correct."

"Greene knows what we're doing. He caught me in the medical sector. He'll be watching us closely. We need to be careful."

"Two walls have fallen. That should keep him occupied. Fortunately for us, he can't have his eyes on everything."

Alan glanced up at the cameras. "But he *can* have his eyes on a whole heck of a lot."

The door swung open, and Charlotte walked in. "I see you all found your way back to the room. It must be difficult learning the layout of this building."

"It is," Alan said. "I got lost more than I like to admit."

"It happens to all of us that are new to the Spire. You're doing quite well. You've only been here a couple days. Some people take weeks to learn their way around."

"I wouldn't say we've learned our way around. We've just been…lucky."

"It's quite easy actually, once you've learned our system. Everything is color coded. I'm sure you've seen the maps on our walls. They're located at every turn, and they're interactive. Just touch where you want to go and it will get you there. It's very user-friendly."

"Yes, we saw those," Ella said. "We didn't know what they were or how to read them."

"You'll learn in time, but until then, Greene is calling a meeting in an hour. He wants to address the wall. I assume they've kept you up to date on the current events."

"Yes. The second wall has fallen."

"It has, and it has never happened before. The first wall has two gaps now. We are more vulnerable than we've ever been. I'm sure Greene wants to calm the people."

"And come up with a plan," Alan said. "He seems like a man who always has a plan. And if his plan doesn't work out, he moves right on to the next one."

"He likes to be prepared," Charlotte said. "That's why he has cameras everywhere. It's impossible to keep up with him. He's always one step ahead of you."

"I can respect a man with a plan," Vince said.

Saul shook his head as if to say, *You respect him?*

Vince acknowledged that Greene was not a man to respect. He was a man to fear. In front of the others, especially Charlotte, he wanted to keep up the act. "I like to be prepared myself, though it isn't always easy."

"Greene makes it look easy," Charlotte said. "He always has a plan."

As she repeated this sentence, the tone of her voice shifted. She knew why they were here, that they intended to kill Greene. Greene knew as well. Was invading Snow Peak his plan, or was there more? How much did Charlotte know? With these questions floating around, one thing was for sure. Dealing with a man so meticulous, they needed to tread lightly.

TWENTY-THREE

GREENE'S MEETING WAS not as big as the conference. He held it in the briefing room, with only a few Spire employees. On the wall behind him was a pinned up banner with the City logo. His suit was freshly cleaned, his hair was combed back, and a touch of makeup brightened his face. He grinned at the camera near the back of the room, and then at his workers. "As you all know, this will be recorded and broadcast across the City. News has spread of the second wall falling. People are looking for answers and that's exactly what I'll give them. Now, let's begin." He cleared his throat and signaled to the camera.

"Good evening, citizens. Victor Greene here, broadcasting from the Spire. As most of you know, today has been very eventful. It is a day that saddens my heart, but also gives me hope. Today marks the first time in the history of the Spire that the second wall has fallen. Simon's attacks are strong and frequent, but don't let that scare you. The Spire is a great place with even greater people. We will band together and stop him from spreading his fear and terrorizing the innocent. We cannot let a man get away with sacrificing innocent children to further his cause. That is unacceptable. We will rise up out of the ruins of the wall and build it back up even stronger, because that's how we deal with terrorists. We don't negotiate. We don't surrender, we fight. We fight until we no longer can. As long as Simon is out there, we will fight for the people of the City." He leaned towards the camera. "Simon, if you're watching, and I know you are, be afraid."

The camera cut and the chatter in the room grew. Greene nodded his head, satisfied with the broadcast, and took a seat at the head of the table. The man to his right held out his hand. "I must say, sir, that was an excellent speech. People were uneasy after the attacks, but you have just put them all at ease." A hum of agreement filled the room.

Greene grasped his hand with a firm grip. "Thank you, Marco." He turned to the others. "Thank you all for your support. With your continued enthusiasm, I know we can get through these tense times. I have devised a plan, and if you follow my orders, I know we will succeed."

They leaned forward, eager to hear his plan. Even Vince and Saul found themselves curious.

"Up until this point, we have been defensive, waiting for Simon to attack. If we keep this up, our last wall will fall, and I'm afraid the Spire will as well. Instead, we must take the offensive. I have many agents working undercover. We know exactly where his camps are. That's a good starting point, but we're not going to run in guns blazing. We already have men inside, so a stealthier approach is the way to go. With their help, we can infiltrate his main base."

He held up a map. "From recently acquired information, it looks like their main base is here. That is where Simon will be. Our mission is to take him out. Anything less will be a failure." He lowered the map. "Simon is not the subtle type. He makes big, explosive moves. If he tries something, we'll know." He looked to Vince and Saul. "These two, guided by Charlotte, will infiltrate the base. I have handpicked one of my best soldiers to go along with you. He will arrive tomorrow, along with the other troops. All others will stay here and guard the walls. We are taking the offensive, but we can't be careless. We must defend the walls well, especially the weak spots."

Vince and Saul shared a glance. Greene was handing them a lot of responsibility. He had confidence that they would comply, that he had scared them into obedience. That was partly true, but they were stronger than that. They still intend to kill him, but for now, they would play along.

Greene looked at them. "The two of you have seen his base before. It's where you first met Simon. You should recognize it. That's why I'm putting you in charge. The element of surprise is key, so stay hidden. Once you're inside you will meet an inside man. He will help you find your way around. People won't recognize you as long as your face is hidden. If things go smoothly, you'll reach Simon unnoticed. Get close to him, and take him out with this." He revealed a small capsule and placed it on the table. "This is a strong toxin. It is very deadly. Ingesting only a small amount can kill you. It has a delayed effect, so you'll have plenty time to get out.

"It's important that you're the ones to kill him. The Heroes of the Spire striking down Simon. A symbolic triumph for all of us, and a devastating blow for the Crowns. I will provide you with earpieces, and watch from the Spire. I will give you direction if needed. If you have any questions, you will have a microphone strapped to your shirt. Use it sparingly. You don't want to draw attention to yourselves."

He paused, running through the plan in his head. "I believe that's everything. You will meet the troops tomorrow. I assure you they're the top of the top, and extremely loyal. They follow orders without hesitation and I expect you to do the same. After you meet them, you will have a short period to rest. Then at sundown, you deploy. The dark will keep you hidden, but once you're below ground, the tunnels are well lit. Keep your faces concealed and act normal. Blend in as one of them."

Vince nodded. "This is a good plan. We will do our best to follow your orders, word for word."

He glared at Saul, who read his message loud and clear. "That's right. You're the boss. Just say the word."

Greene smiled. "That's good to hear. You two are valuable assets. Keep it up."

"What about us?" Alan asked. "What can we do?"

"That is a very good question. *They* will be down there, but I want you to stay up here. This is a stealth mission. I want to keep the group small. There's no room for three more. Instead, if you really want to help, you can assist my troops on the wall. They can show you how to use the cannon."

Rupert stepped forward. "Could we get a closer look at the testing facilities? I've become very interested in your procedures. I would like to see the process from start to finish. I would like to see some more of the medical sector as well."

"Of course. I'll have Charlotte show you around, but that will have to wait until after this mission. They leave tomorrow. There's a lot that needs to get done."

"There's no way to see the place sooner?"

Greene looked at him curiously. "You're very eager."

Rupert shrugged. "I'm from Snow Peak. We don't have much technology. I'm fascinated with your testing and the knowledge that comes with it." He also wanted to find Fred, but he didn't mention that.

Greene smiled. "The tests *are* great, aren't they? They've brought so much good to the City, in ways you wouldn't imagine. And we're constantly improving. Some of our new stuff is very impressive." He gave the request some thought. "I glad you've grown an interest in our work. We'll be busy preparing for tomorrow, but you can look around yourself. Just don't go wandering into places you're not supposed to be."

Rupert nodded. "I do apologize for that. It's easy to get lost in the medical sector. It won't happen again."

"Good. There are cameras everywhere, so if you need assistance, just give a wave. Someone will see you. Feel free to walk around as you please. If you want a more formal tour, Charlotte can show you around when she gets back."

"Thank you," Rupert said.

Greene turned back to Vince and Saul. "You two won't have time to explore, I'm afraid. We will be running through this plan more than once. You must know it inside and out. When your man arrives tomorrow with the other troops, you will spend time with him and get to know him. The mission needs to go as smoothly as possible. You will move with precision and purpose. Anything less is unacceptable. This is too important for leniency."

"We completely agree," Vince said. "We will do our best."

Greene scanned the room, moving from face to face. "It sounds like we have a plan. Let's get to it, people."

TWENTY-FOUR

GREENE SPREAD THE map out in front of Vince and Saul. "This is the layout of the surrounding area. It covers about a half mile radius around the Spire." He took a marker and drew a thick line weaving through streets and alleys. "The closest entrance is here, and this is the quickest route. He has men patrolling the streets, so stay hidden. For the most part, we know where they are. We have plenty of cameras to locate them, but it's still a good idea to stay hidden."

The marker squeaked as he circled the entrance. "This is where you'll meet my inside man. He'll let you in." He pulled out another map, this one showing the tunnel system. Trails split off into complex paths, intersecting at random. Again, he drew a path with the marker. "This is the route you will take. He should know where to go, so just follow him. Make sure to keep up. He moves fast. If you lose him, you'll be left to find your way out on your own."

Saul looked up. "If we get lost you can just tell us where to go, right?"

"We'll try, but our cameras are limited down there. There are a few that are well hidden, but Simon has disabled the rest. In the tunnels, your sight will be handicapped, but once you reach the main area, we have plenty of eyes to keep watch. Simon's lower ranks aren't allowed in the tunnels, so you must be extremely careful. If you are seen, your cover is blown, but once you get to the main area, you should be fine. All Crowns can wander the lower floors. There are no rank requirements so it will be easier to blend in. Just make sure to keep your faces covered. Use these bandanas. It's common for people to cover their mouths down there. The air is not the cleanest. Everyone in the City knows your face, so it's critical nobody sees it.

"My inside man will bring you to the upper floor, but you're on your own from there. He doesn't have access to the area. It's too risky to have him walking around up there. If this mission goes sour, I can't afford to blow his cover. The upper floor will be tricky. Our cameras up there are limited as well, and there are fewer shadows to hide in. Guards patrol the area, but my men have studied their patterns. There is a small opening precisely at sundown when they change shifts. Then, and only then, will you make your move.

"Don't linger. You don't want to stay too long. If the guards come back while you're still around, the mission's over." He slid his finger along the map and stopped near the middle. "This is where you will go. It's the upper-level kitchen, where Simon's personal chef cooks. You will slip the capsule into his food. It is highly soluble, so it should dissolve quickly. Stir it to make sure.

"Once his food is poisoned you will leave immediately. You don't want to be around when he dies. If this mission succeeds, we will announce to the City that you were responsible. We'll tell them that the Spire's two heroes have taken down Simon and saved the people. They'll love you even more than they do already." He looked into their eyes. "And then you're free to go. You can live the rest of your days as free men, doing what your heart desires, until the day you die."

Saul lowered his head, reminded of his own mortality.

Vince saw tears form in Saul's eyes. He found himself thinking of mortality as well. It was hard to accept that his best friend was dying. They were not immortal.

Surprisingly, this frightened him. He did not expect fear, but in the shadow of his fading friend, he was terrified.

Greene saw the fear in both of them. "I apologize for upsetting you. That was not my intention."

Saul did not respond.

"It's a sensitive subject," Vince said. "He just received the news this morning."

"I realize that, and I'm sorry I brought it up." He looked to Saul. "I can only imagine what you're going through. It's one of the things I fear most. That's why I test. To improve life. To make it better. Make it last longer." He gently placed his hand on Saul's shoulder, almost expecting him to shake it off. He did not. "You have lived a good long life. You've seen many things. Accomplished so much. You should be proud. Don't dwell on the end of good memories. Celebrate them."

Saul kept his head down, staring at the map. He did not say a word.

"Very well," Greene said, standing from his seat. "We've covered enough for now. I'll give you some time alone." He walked towards the door. "We can take this up again tomorrow morning." He left.

Charlotte was watching from the corner. She saw sorrow in Saul's face. Her eyes shifted to Vince and saw the same. "Are you two alright?"

Vince sighed. "It's just been a long day. So much is happening. *Too* much."

She nodded. "I've watched you two for a long time. You've been through a lot. More than any person should ever experience. I understand why you hate Greene so much."

"It's not easy to be around him. To work with him." He rubbed Saul's back in an attempt to comfort him. "No matter how much we convince ourselves that Simon is the greater evil, we can't forget everything Greene has done to us."

"Do you think you're just scared? Greene gave you life. You would have died a long time ago, but you got a small taste of immortality, and ever since you learned it's not sustainable, you've been clinging on to life with every muscle in your body. You're scared of death. Scared of the idea that one of these days, you will no longer exist. And this fear is steering your blame towards Greene. You're using him as an excuse to drain. You've convinced yourselves that you have to stop him, and draining lets you do that, but what happens when you succeed? When Greene is dead, will you stop? Will you welcome death, or will you find another excuse?"

Tears ran down Vince's face. "None of that matters. Saul is going to die whether he drains or not."

"That's why I ask." She focused on Saul. "Hey, look at me." He didn't move. "Saul. Look at me." His head tilted up and his eyes found hers. "Do you want to spend your final days in fear? Fearing death? Fearing whatever comes after? If you do, then go ahead. The other option is to accept that death is a part of life. Everyone dies."

"Not us," he whispered.

"Yes, even you. You need to accept that and enjoy every last moment you have. Because what's the point in living if you're scared the whole time?"

Saul looked away and lowered his head again.

She walked to the door. "Death can be a beautiful thing. Just as beautiful as life." She left the room, leaving them with poetic words that only confused them further.

TWENTY-FIVE

RUPERT, ELLA, AND Alan wandered down the hall. This time, they knew how to use the maps displays. Ella touched it. A soft beep played from the speaker, and the display read, *Tap Your Destination*. A long list of floor numbers filled half of the screen. She looked at Rupert. "Where to?"

Rupert combed his hand through his thick beard. "I suppose we should have a system. We've already started this floor. Let's finish it off before moving on."

She tapped *Level 149*. The list of numbers disappeared and a floor plan took its place. Again, she looked to Rupert.

He shrugged. "How about the medical testing labs? They're right next to where we were before."

She tapped the screen, and another soft beep played, followed by an arrow pointing to the left. "I guess we go that way," she said.

"Charlotte was right," Alan said. "That was easy."

They walked a long hall until they reached another wall. Ella went to push the display, but an arrow appeared before she could. This time, it pointed right. They looked up and saw the camera above the map.

Alan crossed his arms and nodded his head. "Now isn't that handy. They know exactly where we are and where we're going."

They followed the beeps and arrows until they arrived at the entrance. There was a set of double doors with the words *Testing Labs* on them.

"Is this where Charlotte brought us before?" Ella asked.

"I think so," Rupert answered. "It looks familiar."

They stared at the door for a moment, until Alan finally walked forward. "What are we waiting for? Let's go." He pushed through and entered the next hallway.

Glass walls stood on either side of them. They saw the same people in the rooms, wearing the same torn rags. Ella watched the same skinny old man she had seen before. He shivered in the corner as a man in a lab coat walked towards him. "Those men creep me out," she said. "What did Charlotte call them? Labbies?"

"Yeah, I think so," Alan said. "I agree. Something feels off about them. It's like they're hiding something."

"That's why we're here," Rupert said. "I'm certain they're hiding something, and we're going to figure out what."

Ella pressed her hand against the glass and looked at the camera in the corner. "How are we going to do that? They're watching everything we do. We can't just go into the restricted area like we did last time."

"Why not? There's nothing stopping us. We just have to be quick and find what we need before they kick us out."

"How much time do you think we'll have?" Alan asked. "They already caught us once. They're probably watching us very closely."

"I don't know about that," Rupert said. "Everyone's busy preparing for tomorrow, especially Greene. He's down there briefing Vince and Saul right now. We may have more time than you think."

Ella nodded. "You're right. It's worth a shot. We need to find Fred."

Alan nodded as well. "If both of you agree, then I'm in too." He walked midway down the hall to the door that read, *Restricted.* "I'm ready when you are."

"We'll have to be careful," Rupert said. "We don't know what's on the other side of that door. Greene may be busy, but the workers aren't on alert anymore. It won't be empty like it was the other day. If anyone see us, they'll kick us out."

Ella looked back to the labbie on the other side of the glass. He was looking down at his clipboard, vigorously writing as he spoke to the patient. "If we're going, we better go now, while they're distracted."

Alan pushed the door open, and the three of them slipped through.

On the other side was another hallway, this one brightly lit. As far as they could see, there was no one around. They snuck down the passage and peeked around the corner. The hall continued, with doors branching off the sides.

"Those must be the back doors to the glass rooms," Ella whispered. She pointed to the first one on the right. "That's the one I was looking in. The one with the labbie."

"For all we know there's a labbie in all of them," Rupert said. "We have to be careful choosing which doors to open."

"So where do we go?"

Alan pointed up at the camera above their heads. "Wherever we go, we better go fast. We've already passed two cameras. They definitely know we're here. We can't just sit around."

Rupert started walking down the path on the left. "This way's as good as any, right?"

They followed him, tiptoeing past the doors and hearing the labbies as they passed each one.

A door opened down the hall in front of them. They froze in place, darting their eyes back and forth to find a place to hide. There was nothing. They stood out in the open, in the middle of the brightly lit corridor. A man in a lab coat walked out, guiding a patient with his arms. He turned left, away from them, and walked the other way. The patient looked back as he walked, and saw the three standing like statues.

Their hearts stopped. Alan raised a finger to his mouth, pleading for him to stay quiet. The man saw his signal, nodded, and turned around as the labbie guided him around the corner.

They sighed with relief. "That was too close," Alan said. "That patient was looking out for us. He's got something against the Spire maybe?"

"Perhaps," Rupert said, "but we may not be so lucky next time. We need to get out of this main hallway. There are too many occupied rooms. Anyone could come at any time. It's too risky."

Alan nodded. "You're right, but where do we go?"

"Let's follow them," Ella said. They both looked at her like she was crazy. "They just came out of the glass room. They're probably not headed to another one. They must be going somewhere else. There's no reason for the labbie to turn around. He won't see us if we're quiet. As long as we keep our distance, they should lead us somewhere important. Or at least somewhere new. I'm getting sick of all of these hallways."

"That sounds like a solid plan to me," Alan said.

Rupert nodded and took the lead, creeping up to the corner and poking his head out. There was a door. He cracked it open and peeked through. It was another long hallway. The two men were nearly at the opposite end already. He signaled to the others and pushed through.

They kept the two men in sight, following their every turn through a maze of the same halls and doors, until finally they reached something different. It was another door, but this one was different. It was larger and made of metal. The labbie held his eye up to a device by the door. A soft beep played over the speakers, followed by the loud clank of metal. The door slid up, and they walked through.

Ella scurried forward. "Hurry, before it closes."

They ran as quietly as they could and slipped under the door just as it was closing. Another loud clank rang through the room as the metal hit the ground.

Alan looked up in awe, stunned by what he saw. "What is this place?"

The hall opened up to a vast room with numerous floors. They looked down into the hollow area. The huge chamber carried catwalks along the sides. Metal cages lined the walls, like prison cells. A single source of light beamed down from the large glass ceiling and down the center shaft, filling the void between the catwalks. The labbie escorted the patient further down the path and into one of the cells.

"I guess the glass rooms are just for show," Alan said. "These are their real rooms."

They stood near the top floor, staring into the dark abyss. Posted on the wall was a sign. It listed each floor and their corresponding sector. *Level 149 – Rehabilitation Sector.* Above that, *Level 150 – Victor Greene.* They looked up and saw a glass viewing room, where Greene could stand and watch over his prisoners. It was currently empty.

Ella looked to Rupert. "What do we do now? If Greene finds out we've seen this, what will he do?"

"He probably already knows we're here," Rupert said. "There's no turning back now. Fred might be in here. I want to look."

Ella and Alan agreed, but as they began to walk, they bumped into a labbie. The same labbie they were following.

"What? Who are you?" he asked, clearly flustered. "How did you get in here?"

They didn't respond.

"This is a restricted area. Only lab technicians and guards are allowed. I'm afraid I must ask you to leave." He motioned to the door. "Here, I'll escort you out. These halls can be a little confusing." He went to the door and held his eye to the device. The door slid open like it did before, and slammed shut once they were through. They walked back through the blank white halls. "I apologize for kicking you out like this, but I could get in trouble. Mr. Greene is very strict about his rules. He has a low tolerance for people who break them. I hope you understand."

"Of course," Rupert said. "What was in there, anyway? I've never seen such a big room before."

"I'm afraid I can't tell you. Sworn to secrecy. Mr. Greene's orders."

"Aww, come on," Alan nagged. "You got to give us something. We have so many questions. We've never seen something so magnificent outside of the City."

The labbie looked at him curiously. "Outside of the City?" His eyes lit up. "Are you with Vince Vigo and Saul Shepherd?"

"We sure are," Ella said with a smile. "Came over on a raft from a place called Snow Peak."

"I can't believe it! I'm actually speaking with people who know the Heroes of the Spire!"

Alan chuckled. "That title has really stuck, huh?"

"It sure has. People can't get enough of those two, especially here in the testing labs. They remind us why we do what we do. To help people. The fact that they came all this way to thank Mr. Greene, it's inspiring. Tell me, what are they like in person?"

Alan shook his head. "Now I don't think that's fair. You have to tell us something about that room first. Then you'll hear all about how great Vince and Saul are."

The labbie hesitated. "I don't know. I'm really not supposed to say anything. He would probably throw me in there with the rest of them if he ever found out."

"He'll throw you where?" Rupert said.

The labbie grew flustered again. "Oh man, I shouldn't have said that." His face turned bright red.

"It's okay," Ella said. "You can tell us. We won't tell anyone else."

"And we'll get you a private meeting with Vince and Saul if you do tell us," Alan said, nudging his arm.

His head turned, and his eyes widened. "A private meeting? With the Heroes of the Spire?"

"That's right, and all you have to do is tell us what that room is. No one needs to know. It's our little secret. Right, guys?"

Ella and Rupert nodded.

They could see thoughts race through his mind as he tried to make a decision. "Okay. I suppose it can't hurt since you're all such big supporters of Mr. Greene's work already."

"Exactly," Alan said. "we're just eager to learn as much as we can. Get every little tidbit."

The labbie nodded. "Right. See these doors? They lead to the glass rooms, which I'm sure you've seen." He opened a door to a vacant glass room. "This is where we keep our patients. As you can see, it's a spacious area with clean, comfortable furniture. A very pleasant place for a patient." He looked behind his back, just to make sure no one was there. "But these are just for show. The truth is, with the amount of patients we have, it's not feasible to build and maintain so many rooms like this." He shut the door and continued down the hall. "That room back there that you saw is called the cell room. It's where we really keep our patients."

"It looked like a prison," Ella said.

"The living conditions aren't quite as nice, but it's much more cost-efficient. Whenever a group comes along for a tour of the Spire, we bring a few lucky patients up for the day to fill these rooms. That's how we reward good patients."

"And how do you punish the bad?" Alan asked.

"I wouldn't say we punish anyone. We just give incentives for good behavior."

"I have a falcon," Rupert said. "Is there any chance she's in there?"

"Is she a patient?"

"She was a patient in the medical sector. They were fixing up her wing."

"No, the medical sector is separate from the rest of them. They keep all of their stuff in their part of the building."

"She wasn't there."

The labbie shrugged. "I couldn't tell you where they brought her, but the cell room doesn't have medical patients. She would only be in there if they were doing tests on her."

They reached the main hallway, outside of the glass rooms. "Well, this is where I'll leave you. How will we arrange my meeting with Vince and Saul?"

"What's your name?" Alan asked. "They're pretty busy right now, but we can have Greene call your name when they're free."

"My name's Humphrey. Humphrey Jacks."

Rupert held out his hand. "It's nice to meet you, Humphrey. Thanks for the information. We appreciate your honesty. We'll make sure you get your meeting with Vince and Saul."

Humphrey gripped his hand and shook with enthusiasm. "Thank you so much. You have no idea what this means to me. Meeting the Heroes of the Spire. The others will be so jealous. Anyways, goodbye." He waved and shut the door.

As they left the testing labs, Ella noticed a worried look on Rupert's face. "What are you thinking?"

"He said they only hold test subjects in the cell room. I'm thinking she's in there. They're doing tests on her, and I'm thinking they're bad ones."

"How do you know they're bad?" Alan asked. "From what I can tell, there are a lot of good tests too."

"They're hiding it from us," he said. "Hidden is always bad."

TWENTY-SIX

THEY ALL HAD trouble sleeping that night.

Vince and Saul's thoughts lingered around Greene's plan of espionage, and Saul's impending death. Vince had thought about Charlotte's words. Was he scared of death, and just using Greene as an excuse? When the time came, would he be able to stop draining? His friend's impending death forced him to think these thoughts. It made his head spin. He could only imagine what Saul was going through.

Saul had chased the possibility of immortality. No matter how weak their powers were, he held on to the belief that he could live forever. That he *would* live forever. Vince had once thought the same. Maybe he still did. But that hope was now gone for Saul. He knew he would die, and he was frightened as hell.

Rupert, Ella, and Alan's thoughts were overwhelmed by what Humphrey had told them about the cell room. Rupert couldn't stand to be apart from Fred any longer. A part of him knew that she was okay. She was a strong bird. She could handle anything. But the other part of him was terrified of the possibility that they were testing her. Terrified that she was locked up in that prison. He needed to find her, to make sure she was safe, but there was nothing he could do. The doors were locked at night, and they were already on thin ice with Greene. There was no doubt that Greene knew they had found the cell room. Either he saw it himself through the cameras, or one of his workers informed him. How would he handle this information? How would he punish them for disobeying orders?

Charlotte slept beside them, in a bed near the door. She had escorted Vince and Saul for nearly their entire stay in the Spire. She had heard them talk about Greene as an enemy. She understood why they loathed him, but she had always looked up to him. She respected him. She overheard conversations to plot against Greene, plans to kill him once Simon was out of the picture, and she did not know what to think of it.

Greene was the man who kept the City in order. Without him, how would it survive? Would it thrive, or crumble? There was only one way to find out. When the time came, would she let them turn on her boss, or would she sabotage their plans? If they failed, they would surely be killed. Her assignment would end, and she would receive a big paycheck. She could retire for the rest of her life. If they succeeded, she had no idea what would happen. For now, she delayed her decision, and instead, recorded everything in her journal. Every spoken word.

None of them knew what would come, but they were all certain, bad things awaited.

TWENTY-SEVEN

IN THE MORNING, with Charlotte busy flipping through her journal, the group met to discuss their plan for the day.

"After the meeting this morning," Vince said, "Saul and I will stay close to Greene. We'll keep him busy. That will give you more time to explore."

Saul nodded. "You found some good information last night. That cell room sounds like it's worth looking into."

"You can thank Humphrey for that," Alan said.

"Who?"

"He was the labbie who told us about the cell room. You guys owe him a meet-up by the way."

Ella laugh. "Yeah, sorry about that. We had to persuade him somehow."

Vince nodded. "Good work. It paid off. We can find some time later on. His name is Humphrey?"

"Yep," Alan said. "Humphrey Jacks. When you meet with him, you can dig for more information. He was pretty hooked when we mentioned your names. I imagine you'll be much more persuasive."

"Perhaps, Vince said. "In the meantime, learn as much as you can about the cell room."

"Right," Rupert said. "I have a growing suspicion that Fred is in one of those cells. I intend to find her. I take it Greene already knows we found the cell room yesterday, so it might be best that we don't attend the meeting this morning. I want to avoid him for as long as we can. Until he stops us, we're going to explore as much as possible."

"Good. Saul and I will be busy most of the day. We may not see you again before we head out, so good luck."

Alan patted him on the back. "You too, buddy."

Charlotte clapped her journal closed, checked the time, and got up from her seat. "It's time for our morning meeting," she said, walking towards them.

"These three aren't feeling well," Vince said, pointing to Rupert, Ella, and Alan. "Is it okay if they skip the meeting?"

"That should be fine, but it's important that you two attend. You're at the center of his plan right now. Without you, there's no mission."

"Right. Of course."

They followed her to the briefing room. They had been there so many time, Vince could have found it with his eyes closed. The rest of the Spire was a mystery.

Greene and the others were already there as they strolled into the room. He was beginning to recognize their faces, but he didn't know any of their names.

They took a seat at the table, and Greene stood up at the front. "Good morning, everyone. I hope you all got a good night of sleep. You're going to need the energy. I don't want anyone falling asleep on this mission."

Everyone laughed.

"This meeting will be short. As you know, our troops return today. They will arrive in the afternoon if everything goes as planned. That gives me enough time to brief them. As I said before, most of them will go on the wall. One will go with Vince, Saul, and Charlotte to help them sneak into Simon's base. Most of you in this room will be their eyes. You will watch the cameras with vigilance and warn them of anything that threatens the mission. I will personally watch over you as well. This mission is a big deal, and requires my undivided attention." He shifted his eyes back and forth, scanning the room. "Where are your friends?"

"They're not feeling well," Vince said "They decided to skip the meeting. I hope that's okay."

Greene nodded. "Very well. I would like to speak with them soon, though, regarding other matters. That will have to wait until tomorrow."

"I will let them know."

"Good. I think we all know what needs to be done today before sundown. So let's get to it." They all stood up and broke off in their own direction. Greene pushed in his chair and walked directly to Vince and Saul. "Are you two ready?"

"I hope so," Vince said. "There's a lot at stake."

"That's right. No room for error. You should know this plan like your life depends on it. There's a good chance it does. If Simon captures you, I have no doubt he'll kill you. He has no reason to keep you alive, and every reason not to. I will be watching very closely. If you have any doubts at all, just follow my direction." He leaned in closer and lowered his voice to a whisper. "And if you disobey me, your friends are dead." He leaned back and returned to his normal speaking voice. "Just listen to my word and I'll guide you. Easy as that."

They were shocked by his sudden change in tone, but did not react. They just nodded, acknowledging his orders.

"Now follow me," he said, walking towards the door. "We'll get you both suited up with all of the necessary equipment."

They followed him to the storage area, where all sorts of gadgets sat around. Uniforms, lab coats, bed sheets, silverware, canned food. In the corner, locked in a cage, were racks full of guns and ammunition. Vince and Saul stared at it, both amazed and frightened. After their incident with Barnabus, the sight of one gun was terrifying enough.

Greene pulled their attention away from the stockpile of weapons by handing them small earpieces. "Stick those in your ear and test them out. Make sure they work okay." They did as he said. He held a small microphone up and tapped on it. "Do you hear that?" They nodded. He turned his back to them and whispered into the microphone. "Do you hear me?"

"Yes," Saul said. "We hear you."

Greene looked at Vince, who nodded in agreement.

Next, he handed them their own microphones. "You will use these to speak with me if you have to, but I will do most of the talking. Only speak back if it's necessary. You don't want to draw attention to yourselves."

Saul held it up to his mouth. "Hello?"

"Yes," Greene said. "It works, but you don't have to hold it so close, and you don't need to speak so loud. Clip it to your shirt and speak normally. That's how they're designed."

He clipped it to the collar of his shirt. "Hello?"

Greene nodded. "Very good." Next, he reached into a small box and pulled out a capsule. "This is the pill you will drop in his food. As I said before, it will dissolve. Just make sure it mixes well." He grabbed another one. "I'll give one to each of you, in case you get separated. Our plan is very precise, but sometimes things go wrong."

Saul laughed. "I think we both learned that a long time ago. Things never seem to go as planned."

"If things do go wrong, I want you to get out of there. We can always try again later, but not if you two get captured. If there are any signs of failure, I will abort the mission. And remember, what I say goes. No questions asked. You both know what's at stake. I can't have anyone acting against me."

Vince nodded. "Yes, we understand."

"I think I've covered everything. The troops will arrive soon. In the meantime, we'll head back to the briefing room, and you can study those maps. Remember as much as you can. You won't have time to fumble through the tunnels once we've started."

TWENTY-EIGHT

VINCE AND SAUL stood at Greene's side as they waited in the lobby for the troops. The front doors opened, and a line of uniformed men filed through. They wore almost entirely black, with the City crest embroidered on their chest. They shuffled in, each carrying a gun by their side. Vince noticed their height. They were all very tall, easily towering over him and Saul. Some of them were even taller than Rupert.

They marched up to Greene and saluted. Greene returned a salute of his own. "Welcome back. I hope all went well on your mission."

The man in front spoke. "Everything went according to plan. The supply shop was secured and Simon's forces were driven out."

"Good," Greene said, satisfied. "You are very much needed around here, as I'm sure you've heard."

"Yes, sir. We are here to serve. What are your orders?"

Greene looked among the troops. "Where is Tully Sanders?"

From near the back of the squad, a voice called out. "Right here, sir!"

"Please step forward," he ordered. The man stepped out of line and turned to face Greene. "Sanders, I have a special mission for you. You are assigned to a stealth operation alongside Vince and Saul." He gestured to both of them. "You will assist these men in assassinating Simon Hedcrown."

"Yes, Sir!"

"You will leave at sundown. Come forward and meet the members of your team. The rest of you are assigned to wall duty."

They all chanted in unison, "Yes sir," and marched out the door towards the wall.

Tully stayed behind. He extended his arm out to Vince. "Tully Sanders. Pleasure to meet you."

Vince shook his hand and introduced himself. Saul did the same.

"You should get to know each other," Greene said. "You should always know a little about the people you work with."

"I already know about Vince and Saul," Tully said. "I reckon everyone knows them by now. I'm honored to work with men who have such dedication to Mr. Greene."

Greene turned to them. "Tully here is one of my top performers. He continues to impress me with both his bravery and loyalty."

Tully saluted again. "Who else would I follow, sir? You're the best leader a soldier could ask for."

Greene chuckled. "And as you can tell, he spoils me with flattery."

Vince nodded at Tully. "I'm sure you already know much about us. We look forward to learning more about you. He must really trust you. He handpicked you for this mission."

"He's the best of the best," Greene said. "Now that we have introductions out of the way, let's get to business. We don't have much time before sundown."

TWENTY-NINE

THEY LEFT THE Spire promptly at sundown. Vince and Saul had thoroughly studied the maps, but Tully and Charlotte already seemed to know their way through the maze of buildings surrounding the Spire. They weaved in and out of the streets, sticking to shadows when they could. They encountered one Crown on patrol, but with Greene looking over them, he was easy to avoid.

When they reached the building marked on the map, Vince and Saul looked at each other. It was the same entrance that Simon's man, Jonah, had brought them through.

They approached the door and knocked lightly five times, in a distinct pattern. It swung open, and a man stepped through.

"Quickly, come in," he whispered. They shuffled inside and shut the door. The man huddled close to them. "Follow me as quickly and quietly as possible. We have to move fast."

They did as he said and gently trotted behind him as he navigated through the tunnels. He turned onto branching paths more than a dozen times before passing an area with a single television screen in the middle.

Saul stopped and whispered to the others. "Hey, isn't it this way? This is where Simon took us last time."

Their guide backtracked. "That way will lead to the main floor, but only Simon and few others are allowed in here. That's a high-profile entrance. Someone might notice. I know a way that's far less conspicuous."

They took a few more turns and arrived at an old rusty door. The man leaned on the door, pushing until it finally budged. The hinges screeched, and the bottom scraped the concrete ground. It stopped with just a small crack to slip through. They squeezed between the door and the wall and carefully shut it behind them. Their guide began to walk again, but his stride was now more casual. They exited an alley and entered the main floor.

Crowds of people wandered the area, leisurely strolling along.

"Okay," he said, "we're no longer in a restricted area. We don't need to whisper anymore, but keep your faces hidden." He pointed to Vince and Saul, who pulled the bandana over their mouths. They walked into the main square, which was filled with a dense crowd of people. "Stay close and keep up. I don't want to lose you." He stepped into the crowd.

They bumped shoulders with strangers as they shuffled through a wave of people. No one paid any attention to them, but they kept their heads low just in case. Tully watched the back end of the group, gripping the hidden gun under his cloak. If anything went wrong, he was ready.

They passed by the statue of Harry Hedcrown. Vince and Saul stopped to admire it. It was surreal to see the man from their hometown, the man who was famous for his brilliant mind. His brilliance had followed him all the way to the City. People gathered around, enjoying the sight of the man who started the Crowns. Some even knelt down and prayed to him.

"Hey!" Greene said into their ears. "The two of you need to keep up. Stay with the group. We're on a tight schedule. You can look at that statue later." The two of them turned around and pushed through the crowd to catch up.

They entered what looked like a marketplace. Various tables were set up, some with small trinkets, others with oily street food. People yelled over each other, calling out prices and handing out merchandise. It was a crowded, bustling mess. If this was how the underground was, Vince couldn't imagine what street level was like during peak hours. They reached the end of the path and looked back and forth to find the others.

"Turn right," Greene said, "and pick up the pace. They're almost at the entrance to the upper levels."

They turned right and moved a little faster. As the crowd began to thin, they walked even faster, picking up speed until they reached a steady trot. Off to the side, they saw Charlotte and Tully. They jogged up and studied the door against the wall.

"Sorry about that," Saul said. "The place is packed. It's easy to get lost in the mix."

"Don't let it happen again," Tully said. "This mission is too important to be fooling around."

Vince and Saul nodded.

Their guide walked up to the door. "This door leads to the upper level. It is much less crowded up there, so you shouldn't get lost, but there will be other concerns. The place is heavily guarded. They follow a strict patrol schedule and their shift change starts in approximately three minutes. That is your one chance to get through. You'll have about ten minutes to get in, poison his food, and get out. Screw up and the mission's over. Do you understand?" They nodded. "Good. This is where I leave you. I can't risk blowing my cover. Once you're in, go straight ahead and then turn left. You'll want to find a bright red tent. That's where Simon's chef will be. You know what to do from there. Be careful. I believe there is some sort of alarm system set up. If you trigger it, they'll be on you in seconds." He raised his hand. "Good luck." He stared at his pocket watch, counting down the seconds. When the hand struck zero, he swung the door open. "Go now."

They dashed through the door and into a small empty courtyard. There were no guards around, just as they had planned. The area split off into five paths.

"I don't have a visual on you," Greene said. "You're on your own."

"Straight and then left," Tully said. "Simple enough. We have ten minutes." He pulled out his own digital watch and pressed the button on the side. A ten-minute countdown began. "We better get moving."

They softly stepped down the path straight ahead. There was no sign of anyone, which made Vince uneasy.

He expected to see at least one person, someone they would have to sneak by, but there was no one.

"This place is empty," Saul said.

Tully hushed him. "That's because they're changing shifts, but that doesn't mean they can't hear you. Keep your voice down.

"He's right," Charlotte said. "We don't have many cameras down here, but I have seen some of the footage that we *do* have. Most of the guards are at the tagging station right now. They take plenty of time tagging out and tagging in, but we can't get too comfortable. You never know, one of them might stray from the group.

Vince darted his head around, making sure that was not the case. "We would be in a lot of trouble if that happened."

"Would you all shut up and focus," Tully whispered. "You'll just draw more attention."

They stopped talking and continued down the path. When they reached the end, they turned the corner and immediately saw the red tent. Tully pulled out his watch again. Six minutes left. He signaled for the others to follow his lead and cautiously approached the back of the tent. There was a back entrance. He pushed through the opening and poked his head in. Humming came from the other side, behind a partition.

"Wait," Saul whispered. He pointed down at the tripwire at Tully's feet. He grabbed Vince and waved the others back. He pulled the capsule from his pocket and held it up. "Wait here," he mouthed. "We'll do it."

Vince shuffled through his pocket for his own capsule.

Tully nodded. "We'll keep watch," he mouthed back.

They carefully stepped over the tripwire and along the side of the tent. Boiling water from behind the divider steamed up and dripped from the ceiling. The alluring aroma filled Vince's mouth with saliva. His stomach began to rumble as he realized how hungry he was. He ignored the smell to focus on his task.

Saul peeked around the corner. There was a man in front of a gas stove, humming a jovial tune. As Saul began to step out, the man spun around, flipping the pot in his hands. Saul swung back behind the barrier, listening to the tune move along the side of the tent. They both stood like rocks, waiting to see where the humming would go. It moved away, back towards the stove, made a sharp turn to the left, and left through the front of the tent. Saul peeked around the corner again. The chef was gone, and the steaming pot remained over the hot flame.

Saul leaned his neck down, towards the microphone. "The guy left the water boiling on the stove."

"Perfect," Greene said. "The capsule will easily dissolve in hot water. It will be virtually undetectable. Drop it in and get out of there."

Vince kept his eyes on the front entrance as Saul stepped towards the boiling water and plopped the capsule in. It floated for a short second and disappeared in an instant. He turned back and gave a thumbs up.

A blaring ring sounded from the top of the tent. Vince and Saul slammed their hands over their ears and ran towards the back. The tripwire was tripped, and both Tully and Charlotte were gone. Charlotte's journal lay on the ground, covered in dust and dirt. They heard the chef, running back into the tent.

"Come on!" Saul yelled, praying that Vince could hear him over the deafening alarm. "Let's get out of here!"

Saul hunched over to pick up the journal and followed Vince, sprinting back from where they came. Behind them, the chef emerged from the tent, shaking his fist in the air. They came to an intersection, but could not remember which way to go. In the chaos, they had both become completely lost.

"Greene!" Vince yelled into his microphone. "We're at the cross! Which way do we go?" There was no answer. "Greene!"

"Damn it!" Saul yelled as guards came running towards them. He grabbed Vince and turned right.

In the distance, they saw the door to the main floor. They dashed with all of their speed, but guards cut them off in front of the door. Guards ahead, and guards behind. They were trapped.

"Don't give up!" Vince yelled. "If they're going to stand in our way, we're going to ram right through them!"

They picked up speed and put their shoulders forward, bracing for impact. They slammed into the guards and toppled over, falling to the ground and scrambling to get back up. Before they could recover, the guards from behind lunged forward and piled on top of them. They struggled to break loose. Vince punched a guard in the neck. Saul kicked a guard in the shin. They both put up a fight, but there were too many. The chef strolled up in front of them, looking down at their faces, which were smothered into the ground. He walked up to Saul and kicked him in the face with his heavy boot. Saul went limp. Vince watched the chef saunter over, his boots clunking on the ground with each step. He raised his foot and slammed it down into Vince's nose.

THIRTY

VINCE OPENED HIS eyes. His blurry vision grew clearer as he blinked. The only thing in sight was an empty wooden chair, sitting directly in front of him. He lay on his side, hands and feet tied behind his back. A tight gag was wrapped around his head and stuffed inside his mouth. He tried to call for help, but his cries were muffled by the saliva-soaked cloth. His eyes darted back and forth. In the corner was a foot. It was Saul. He was tied up and gagged as well. Vince could hear his grunts of desperation.

The sound of leather boots appeared from the end of the room behind them. They grew closer and louder with each step. Saul continued to grunt and moan. The steps moved over to Saul, followed by a sudden thump. He let out a high-pitched whimper and fell silent. Sweat dripped from Vince's brow as the leather boots came into sight. Simon approached the wooden chair and sat down, leaning forward to look at his face. He held a mug of steaming water in his hand.

"It's good to see the two of you. I had a feeling our paths would cross again, though I didn't expect it to be so soon." He sniffed the steam rising from his mug. "Man that smells good. Caleb can really make a good cup of tea." He waved the mug in front of Vince. "Smell that? That's the smell of victory. Smells good, doesn't it?" He pulled it back. "But it's not for you. I think it's pretty clear that you've lost. Greene has sent you to sneak around and spy on me. I can't say I'm surprised. He's always avoided facing me head on like a man. Instead, he devises these schemes to operate behind my back. He thinks it works too, but I know about his agents. He has men planted right under my nose. I know exactly who they are too, but I'm not going to tell him that. I'll just keep on letting him think he has the advantage.

"Now, before you start thinking that Greene is going to save you," he held up their earpiece and microphone, "I've cut all communication with him. As far as he knows, you're dead." He chuckled. "I suppose you will be soon. But not yet. I want to make it public. I want to broadcast your death to the entire City. I want every man, woman, and child to know that the Heroes of the Spire are nothing more than pathetic lab rats."

He patted Vince on the shoulder. "So sit tight. Don't struggle. You might as well relax in your last precious moments of life. Tomorrow it's over." He stood up and walked behind Vince's back. "You know what? I'm feeling generous. Enjoy this nice hot cup of victory." Vince heard the sizzling sound of scolding liquid on skin, followed by a painful grunt from Saul. The mug shattered on the ground, and his footsteps faded in the distance.

Vince tried to position his body to see Saul, who was still whimpering in pain. He rocked back and forth, gaining momentum, when the knot in his gag came undone. He twisted his head until the cloth hung loosely from his neck. "Saul," he said, bending his head back. "Are you okay?"

Saul answered with muffled gibberish.

Vince rolled onto his back, flattening his arms and legs under the weight of his body, and flipped over onto his other side. He saw Saul across the room, tied up just like him, gag and all. His face was glowing red, drenched with steaming hot tea. His forehead was bruised, and his shirt was stained with blood.

"Jeez," Vince said. "They really beat you up. Just stay still. I'll get us out of this." He rocked his body and flipped over again, rolling across the room. With one final push, he plopped down back to back with Saul. He felt around with his hands, looking for the knot around Saul's wrists. When he found it, he viciously tugged away.

Saul's arms and legs came free, falling to the ground beside him. Weak and sore, he carefully rolled onto his back and ripped the gag out of his mouth. He coughed violently and spit a mouthful of saliva onto the ground.

"You didn't swallow any of that tea, did you?" Vince asked.

"I tried not to, but that gag soaked up a lot of it. Do you think that's the water we poisoned?"

"I think so."

"Damn it!" Saul yelled, walking over to untie Vince. "He didn't drink a sip of it. This whole thing was for nothing!"

"Keep your voice down. We don't want them to know we're free."

Saul tilted his head. "Free? We're not free. We're trapped in this room with no way out, and tomorrow that crazy son of a bitch is going to kill us."

Vince stood up, rubbing the irritated skin on his wrists. "Calm down. I'm sure Greene is working up a way to rescue us right now."

"Are you sure about that? It looked to me like his boy Tully ditched us back there."

"Charlotte too?"

Saul shook his head. "No, I don't think so." He reached into his pocket and pulled out her journal. "She wouldn't have left this behind. This is what I think happened. As soon as I dropped that capsule in the water, Greene ordered Tully to trip the alarm. If things had gone the way he wanted them to, Simon would be poisoned, and the Crowns would kill us. Fortunately for us, Simon wants to make our execution public. Somewhat less fortunate for us, he's still alive and well. No poison, no quiet death, and he's going to kill us tomorrow."

"Greene will rescue us. He needs us alive."

"Not if Simon's dead. That's the only reason he needs us, to help against Simon. With Simon out of the picture, he has every reason to kill us."

"You're right. He knows we plan on killing him. The only solution to his problem is to take Simon and us out at the same time. I could turn us into martyrs. Not only will we be the successful subjects he wants, but the men who sacrificed their lives to protect the Spire and everything in it. We would be the symbol he wants, without the threat of keeping us around. He said he would let us free after all of this, but there's no way he could trust us to stay away."

"He has a point. We have no reason to stay away. We would come back and fight even stronger."

Vince nodded. "He knows this. So this little mission was a setup. It was a way to get us out of the picture."

"And what about Rupert, Alan, and Ella?" Saul asked. "If Greene planned this out, he might have plans for them as well."

"Let's just hope that's not the case. We can't do much more than that. Right now, we have to focus on getting out of here. I don't intend to die tomorrow."

Saul searched the ground, felt the walls, and looked up at the ceiling for any signs of escape. "Neither do I."

THIRTY-ONE

THE JOURNAL SLIPPED out of Charlotte's hand as Tully pulled her wrist and dragged her away from the tent. "Wait," she said pulling back, but he was too strong. There was no point in resisting. Even with her strong physical background, Tully was an elite soldier, trained by the best. There was no way she could take him alone.

He led her back the way they came as the alarm went off behind them. They exited back to the main floor, where Greene's man was waiting.

"Everything go well?" he asked.

Tully nodded. "Just as we planned."

"Good. Mr. Greene will be pleased."

"Mr. Greene ordered this?" Charlotte asked with surprise. "Why would he do that? Why didn't he tell me?"

"Don't take it personally," Tully said. "The two of us are the only ones who knew. Everyone else was in the dark just like you."

"We can't just leave them back there," she said, pulling the door handle.

Tully leaned on the door, keeping it closed. "It's Mr. Greene's orders. Let them drop the poison, and then trip the alarm."

"But why?"

"You know why. It's all in that journal of yours."

She searched her body. "Huh, I must have dropped it back there. We have to go back and get it. I can't lose my journal."

"We can't go back. That place is swarming with guards by now."

"You don't understand. A monitor agent must never lose their journal. There are hundreds of years recorded in that book. If I lose it, I'm in big trouble."

"Don't worry, Charlotte," Greene said in her ear. "It's a small price to pay for this successful mission. By tomorrow, two of our problems will disappear. The three people that want to kill me will be dead. Your assignment will be over and the journal won't matter anyway. You'll retire and the Spire will move on to better things. You must be looking forward to your big payday. Every monitor agent does."

"I certainly am sir. I just don't feel comfortable ending my assignment like this."

"You know I had no other choice. Those two put me in a tight position. They're stubborn. They were dead set on killing me once Simon was out of the picture."

"I suppose," Charlotte said as her head slouched towards the ground.

Greene's voice turned soft and sincere. "Charlotte, I may have kept you in the dark, but I made sure Tully got you out of there because you're a valuable part of the team. I look out for my workers. Vince and Saul were not part of our family. They were outsiders. Intruders trying to push their way in and break up a good thing we have going on. They were no good to keep around."

Charlotte nodded. "You're right. I'm sorry I doubted you, sir."

"These are confusing times, I know, but it will all be over soon. Just stick with me until then."

"What about the others?" she asked. "Rupert, Ella, and Alan? What about them?"

"I'll deal with them. They've been sneaking around too much. Exploring places they shouldn't be, like the medical sector, and the cell room. If they want to get into the cell room, I'll make it easy for them. I'll throw them in there with their dumb little bird."

Her head slouched towards the ground again. "Yes, that seems logical."

"I'm glad you see things my way, Charlotte. It would break my heart to throw you in there with them. Now get out before the guards come. I'll be waiting for you here in the Spire."

THIRTY-TWO

RUPERT, ELLA, AND Alan watched from the top of the Spire, as Vince and Saul left on their mission, precisely at sundown. Once they moved past the outer wall and disappeared into the cluster of buildings, Rupert turned around. "Ready?"

Alan nodded. "Ready as ever, boss."

"We're going to the cell room, right?" Ella asked. "How are we getting in?"

"We need to get through that eye scanner. Maybe that labbie can help us."

"Good old Humphrey Jacks," Alan said. "He wasn't the brightest person. Think we can trick him again?"

"I think so. We may even get him to help us find Fred."

"He said he doesn't know where they're keeping her."

"But he *does* know his way around the cell room. He knows how the cells are organized. He'll be helpful, regardless of whether or not he knows where Fred is, as long as we can get him to cooperate."

Alan laughed. "He loves Vince and Saul so much; we could get him to do pretty much anything."

"How do we find him?" Ella asked.

"The medical sector had a computer to call certain nurses. The testing labs must have something similar."

"Great," Alan said, walking towards the door. "Let's go then."

"It's sundown," Ella said. "The labs are empty. He's probably off shift at this hour."

"Right," Rupert said. "In the morning then. In the meantime, let's get some rest." He lay down in bed and let his eyes drift.

*****

He awoke to a gun pointed directly at his face. His heart raced out of his chest as he looked around the room. There were six men, fully armed with military-grade weapons.

"Get up slowly," the man said to Rupert. "No sudden movements."

Rupert did as he said and slowly stood up from his bed. "May I ask what this is about?"

"Mr. Greene has ordered us to arrest the three of you."

"On what grounds?" Ella asked.

"Treason."

"That's ridiculous," Alan said. "We didn't do anything wrong."

Rupert raised his hand. "Easy, Alan. Just let them do their jobs."

They flipped them onto their stomachs and tied their hands behind their backs. They picked them up and walked them out of the room, through the hallways.

"Where are you bringing us?" Alan asked.

"Where we bring all of our prisoners. The cell room. You're going to be locked away for a long time."

Alan sneered. "Vince and Saul aren't going to be happy when they hear about this. Do you hear me?"

The man chuckled. "I guess you haven't heard."

"Heard what?"

"Vince and Saul aren't coming back."

As soon as the words left the man's lips, they passed by a room with a television, and Alan caught a glimpse of the screen. It was a news report. The headline read, *Vince and Saul Captured by Simon. Public Execution Scheduled Today.*

"No," he whispered. "It can't be. They had it all planned out. How could they get captured?"

The man shrugged. "Something must have gone wrong."

"Simon's going to execute them?" Ella asked.

"That's right. Last night he announced it would take place at noon today." He lifted his arm to look at his watch. "It looks like your friends have about three more hours to live."

"Greene has to do something," Alan said. "He has to rescue them, right?"

"He doesn't have anything planned. It's too risky, and there isn't enough time. I'm afraid your friends are out of luck."

Alan struggled. "We have to help them! We have to do something. We can't just stay here and watch."

"I'm afraid that's all I can let you do. Mr. Greene gave us strict orders. You'll be stuck in a cell for a good long while. Although, I suppose there aren't any televisions down there, so you won't have to watch after all." He chuckled, along with the other men.

"Just let us go," Alan continued, as they led them into a restricted area. "Let us try to rescue them. If it's as dangerous as you say it is, you don't have anything to lose. Simon will kill us and you'll have nothing to worry about. Just let us try."

The man shook his head. "Sorry, no can do. Mr. Greene's orders are to lock you up, and that's what I'm going to do."

Alan's head twisted back. "Ella! Rupert! Say something."

They looked at each other and shrugged. There was nothing they could do to help, and they both knew it. They did not have the time or the resources to attempt such a rescue. Charging into Simon's base would certainly get them killed, but going along with these men would get them one step closer to Fred. Rupert shook his head at Alan and continued down the hall with no resistance.

Alan glanced back with amazement and lowered his head. "This is crap," he said.

"Crap indeed," the man said. "You better get used to the smell. Where you're going, it's a pretty crappy place."

After twists and turns through the maze of hallways, they came to the same metal door. The man held his face up to the scanner, and the door slid open.

They walked through the threshold and entered the cell room. It was just as wide and expansive as they remembered. The sunlight shined bright through the glass ceiling, lighting the catwalks. As they passed each cell, they saw men and women huddled away in the corners. The man pushed Alan with his gun. "Come on, move it. This floor is for test subjects only. You're going down to the lower levels."

They reached the stairs and made their way down. Their shoes clanged upon metal with each step, and with each floor they passed, they saw the health of the people deteriorate. The light grew dimmer as the glass ceiling grew farther away. Rupert looked around as they neared the lower levels. The cells no longer held people, but animals. Is this where Fred was locked up? They passed another two levels and reached a sign. *Lower Levels. Proceed with Caution: Prisoners are Dangerous.*

The hisses and shrieks of wild animals quickly transformed into cackles and threats from prisoners. The sunlight was so faint now they could barely see at all. The guards pulled out their portable lights and clicked them on. They glowed a soft hum of artificial light. Alan took another step down the stairs, but the man stopped him. "Hold on, buddy. You're not going that far down. Only Simon's men go down there. You're on this floor."

Alan looked at the number displayed on the wall, *130.* Had they really walked nineteen levels? The men escorted them along the catwalk until they reached three empty cells.

The man opened the door and wave at Alan to move. "Get in."

Alan looked at the others and shrugged. They had no choice. He entered the cell and the man locked the metal bars behind him. Once they were all locked up, the man nodded his head. "Enjoy it down here. You're not going to see much else for a while." He tapped the metal with the tip of his gun and then walked away. The other five men followed.

When they were gone, Alan called out to Rupert's cell. "Now what? We're locked in. We can't help Fred from a cell."

"There must be a way out," Ella called.

"Why would there be? This is the Spire, remember? They have top of the line technology. Why would their prison be anything less than stat- of-the-art?"

"Even the best have their flaws," Rupert said. "I don't know how yet, but we'll get out."

Alan moved to the back of his cell and sat against the wall. "If you say so."

THIRTY-THREE

VINCE SAT AT one end of the room, with his back against the wall. Saul sat across from him. After having examined the chamber, they realized there was no breaking out. The walls and floor were made of thick concrete, and the only door was hefty, with three guards patrolling the other side.

The metal door creaked open, grabbing their attention. Simon entered the room and looked at them sitting against the walls. "Huh, you got loose of your bounds. No matter. You're still here. That's all that matters."

They both stared back at him.

"No final words? Most people curse me out before they're executed. They call me a monster, but I guess that's up to you. It makes things easier for me."

Four other men walked in behind him and grabbed them, lifting them up from the ground. They dragged them out of the room and through a series of tight corridors. Simon followed behind. They entered an open courtyard, the one where the rally was held. The men dragged them up on stage. Two nooses dangled at the center, raised up on two platforms. The huge crowd of people booed and hissed as they crossed the stage, shouting obscenities and throwing trash.

When Simon stepped up behind them, the crowd switched to a loud uproar of cheers. He waved and smiled. "Okay calm down. We'll get to these two in a moment. I know you're all eager, but I ask for you to be patient. I promise, they'll get what they deserve, but first I would like to say a few words."

Before he could continue, the giant screen above the stage cut to static. Simon gritted his teeth. "Christ, not again."

When the picture came back, it showed Greene's office, but it was not Greene in front of the camera. It was a woman. She glanced nervously behind her back and then turned to face the camera. She spoke quickly and with purpose. "Attention people of the City. My name is

Charlotte Marble. I am an employee in the Spire. I have been instructed by Victor Greene to address you on his behalf." She checked behind her back again. "As you know, not too long ago we were visited by Vince Vigo and Saul Shepherd. They were welcomed by Greene, and embraced by all of you wonderful people. We called them the Heroes of the Spire. I am their monitor agent, and I have watched them since the beginning of their journey. I know things about them that no one else knows. I am ready to share what I know because it's very important.

"Vince and Saul are not here for the reasons they say. They do not admire Mr. Greene, and they are not here to thank him. They are here to kill him. These so called *heroes* are traitors. They killed Mr. Greene's most trusted man, and now they're coming for Mr. Greene himself."

The screen cut to footage of Vince shooting Barnabus in the cave, and then back to Charlotte.

"These are the men you idolize. They are a danger to the Spire and a danger to Mr. Greene. We have exposed them for who they truly are, but they have escaped and are currently on the run." Voices came from behind her. She looked around in a panic and whipped her head back to the camera. "If you see them, they must be stopped. They must be killed. Do it for the Spire."

The picture cut out, and then back to the stage. Simon stared at the screen, jaw open, with nothing to say. He looked at the crowd, who stared back at him, waiting for him to speak. He grabbed Vince and Saul and pulled them off stage. "Come with me." He dragged them away from the camera and turned off his microphone. His four guards watched from a distance. "What the hell was that?"

Vince shrugged. "It's true. Every word she said. Just like we told you before, we're here to kill Greene. But you already knew that."

"Then why haven't you done it yet? Why have you been hanging out in the Spire and sneaking around my base? I saw you shake hands with the man. If you hate him so much, why is he still alive?"

"We had no choice," Saul said. "They captured us after the rally and forced us to work with them. He would have killed us if we tried anything."

"Because you don't have the guts," Simon said. "So now what am I supposed to do? I can't kill you. That's exactly what Greene wants."

"We can help you," Vince said. "Just like we agreed on before. We need your help as well. Our friends are still in the Spire. We need to break them out."

"And we still want to kill Greene," Saul added.

"Yeah?" Simon said. "How are you going to help us? We've already breached the second wall. We're doing just fine without you."

"We've been inside," Vince said. "We've seen how they operate and we know their weaknesses. You broke through the second wall, but the same plan's not going to work twice. We can help you form a new strategy."

Simon stared at them, rubbing the stubble on his chin. "Fine, but if we do this, we must convince them it was all planned. I sent you to the Spire to spy on them. If those people believe for one second that I'm working with the enemy, they'll be outraged. They're a wild crowd. You saw how they reacted last time."

"We don't want that again," Saul said. "That's for sure."

"For now, we are allies," Simon continued, "but once all of this is done, you go your own way. Do you understand?"

Vince nodded. "That's reasonable."

Saul nodded as well.

"Good. My men will escort you back to your room. I'll break up this crowd, and then we have some planning to do."

THIRTY-FOUR

CHARLOTTE LOOKED AROUND in a panic and whipped her head back to the camera. "If you see them, they must be stopped. They must be killed. Do it for the Spire."

She hit the button to end the broadcast and jumped up to leave as quickly as possible. As she reached the door, it slid open, and Greene walked in. He shot an accusing glare. "What are you up to?"

"Nothing," she said, startled and by his imposing figure. "Just watching the news. Vince and Saul's execution is on."

"Cut the crap. I know you sent out a broadcast." He looked at the television to see Simon step on stage.

Greene signaled to his guards. "Make sure she doesn't go anywhere." He sat in his chair and watched the screen.

Simon stepped over to the middle of the stage. "I apologize for that little hiccup. I'm afraid our plans have changed. I am ready to reveal something very important." He cleared his throat. "You see, Vince and Saul have been working for the Crowns. I sent them to the Spire as part of a mission. Their cover was only known to me. I wanted to keep it secret. So we put together this mock execution and planned for them to escape, upon which they would return to the Spire. However, it appears that their cover is blown. It is clear from that lady's broadcast that Greene has figured it out. It is unfortunate. They have been of great help sneaking around in the Spire for me. But now, no more secrecy. I will work closely with them to tear down Greene once and for all!"

Greene turned to Charlotte. "Nothing, huh? That sure seems like something to me."

"I—"

"Don't speak to me. Not a single word. You've committed treason. I hope it was worth it. You could have sat back and watched Vince and Saul die. Your assignment would be over and you'd be set for the rest of your life. I would have taken care of you like I take care of all my loyal employees, but now you've condemned yourself to a life in the cell room, rotting behind bars."

"I—"

"What did I say about speaking? Not a single word." He signaled to his guards. "Get her out of here. I've looked at this filth for long enough."

They dragged her out as Greene turned back to the screen. He flipped through the news, listening to reports of Charlotte's broadcast.

Breaking news! Just moments ago a broadcast was sent from the Spire. A lady, claiming to be Vincent Vigo and Saul Shepherd's monitor agent, proclaimed them as traitors, not heroes. Following the broadcast, Simon Hedcrown, leader of the notorious group known as the Crowns, confirmed that he is working closely with these two individuals to take down Victor Greene. People are questioning what this means for the City. If these so called traitors can infiltrate the Spire and shake Victor Greene's hand, really how secure is the Spire? What else don't they know? Does Simon Hedcrown have more men in Victor Greene's administration? The Crowns are gaining momentum, and with the recent attacks on the Spire, citizens are questioning if they are safe. So far, Victor Greene has remained silent. We are all eagerly waiting to hear what he has to say.

He switched off the screen and sighed. "There's always something to fix."

He switched it back on and hovered his finger over the broadcast button, thinking of what to say? His attempt to kill Simon had clearly failed and now his plans for Vince and Saul were awry. They must have figured out he set them up. There was no doubt they would cooperate with Simon going forward. He pressed the button and looked at the camera.

"Greetings citizens," he said, "Victor Greene here to bring you some important news. There are rumors going around that Vince and Saul are traitors to the Spire, and working with the Crowns. Unfortunately, these rumors are true. Charlotte Marble, the lady who sent the last broadcast, recently found some disturbing footage. She immediately brought it to my attention, but by that point, they had already escaped. I commend Charlotte for her excellent work in preventing a potential catastrophe. I want to assure all of you that we have things under control. These terrorists may frighten you, but they are no more than scum and filth. We will find Vince. We will find Saul. We will find Simon. And we will crush them all."

He pressed the button again to end the broadcast and switched back to the news.

So there you have it. Victor Greene has confirmed the rumors. Vince and Saul are not the heroes we thought they were. This is unfortunate news, but Victor Greene has spoken words of strength and reassurance. Let us hope his words are true, that he can keep us safe from these dangerous terrorists. These are scary times indeed, but his confidence gives me hope. It gives all of us hope.

Victor switched it off. "Good enough."

THIRTY-FIVE

A LAN LAID ON his back, looking up at the ceiling. "How long are we going to wait here? Shouldn't we at least try something? Cutting these bars, or breaking these walls? Anything?"

"No," Rupert said. "None of that will work, not in time at least. We need to get out quick, and the quickest way is to find someone with security clearance."

"How about that labbie?" Ella said.

"Yes," Rupert said. "Humphrey Jacks. He is perfect."

"And he's easy to manipulate," Alan said. "He gave up that information pretty easily."

"But we haven't delivered on our promise yet," Ella said. "He hasn't gotten his meeting with Vince and Saul."

Alan laughed. "Well, that's even more reason for him to help us. He can't expect us to set up a meeting if we're locked up."

"What are you guys talking about," Ella said. "Vince and Saul will be dead in a few hours. We can't set up a meeting even if we were free."

Boots clanged on the metal stairs above. "Someone's coming," Rupert said.

They listened as the footstep got closer. The creak of each step hovered just above them. They glared at the stairs, waiting for the person to reveal themselves. Legs came into sight. Then a body. And finally a face. It was Charlotte.

"Charlotte!" Alan yelled. "You came to help—"

Before he could finish, he noticed that her hands were bound. Two guards came down the stairs behind her, guns drawn. They escorted her to an empty cell and locked her inside, before turning around and climbing back up the stairs.

At first, the three said nothing. They stared straight ahead in confusion.

Finally, Alan broke the silence. "If no one else is going to ask, then I will. What the hell happened up there? Why are they locking you up?"

"For saving Vince and Saul's lives," she answered.

"What?" Ella said, letting out a sigh of relief. "Vince and Saul are alive? They weren't executed?"

"No. It was interrupted."

"By what?"

"I sent out a broadcast and said they were traitors, working for Simon to kill Greene. Now he can't kill them."

"Holy crap," Alan said. "So that means they're working with Simon now. Damn, this is getting confusing."

"If they're alive," Rupert said, "that means we can still get Humphrey to help us."

"Vince and Saul are traitors now," Ella said. "Will he still want to meet them?"

"It's worth a shot," Alan said. "We can convince him they're still secretly working for Greene or something. That doof will believe anything."

"Humphrey Jacks?" Charlotte said. "He's not the brightest. It still baffles me how he got his position as a labbie."

"He can get us out, right?"

"He has the authorization, if that's what you're asking. I do too, until tomorrow when they wipe me from the system. But that doesn't do us any good if I'm locked up in this cell, without access to the control room. Humphrey though. He can definitely get us out."

Rupert nodded. "We just need a way to contact him."

"Guards!" Alan yelled. "Guards get over here! It's an emergency!" He waited for a response, but there was nothing. He slapped his knee. "Shucks! Well, it was worth a try. Anyone else got any ideas?"

Charlotte pointed to the small kiosk across from them. A small light was blinking from the bottom panel. "That's a computer. It has a directory of people who work in the Spire. If we can somehow reach it, we can use it to call Humphrey."

"Like the one we saw in the medical sector," Ella said.

"Exactly. Right now I'd say that's our best option."

"And then what?" Alan asked.

"We find Fred," Rupert said, "and then we get the hell out of here."

Charlotte pointed to the kiosk again. "If we can convince Humphrey to let us free, we can use the evacuation pods. I doubt they'll follow us if we shoot out to the water."

"No," Ella said. "We go for Greene first, before we leave."

"Don't push our luck," Alan said.

"If we leave the Spire, we may never get a chance to take him out. We may never see him again. Our alliance with him is already broken, so there's no reason we shouldn't go after him, right? We can deal with Greene, and Vince and Saul can deal with Simon."

"You make it sound so easy."

"Actually," Charlotte said, "it won't be too difficult once we're free of the cell room. Only a small number a people know we're locked up. To everyone else, we're still his allies. Of course, we'll be on camera, but if we make it to the server room, I can shut them all off. Then he'll be blind."

"I like it," Ella said. "We might be able to pull this off."

Rupert stared at the kiosk. "First, we have to figure out how to reach that thing."

They all stared straight ahead, watching the light blink. It was just out of reach.

THIRTY-SIX

A S THEY WAITED for Simon to return, Saul flipped through the monitor journal, fascinated by the idea that his entire life was chronicled in such a small book. He turned the pages and read about past events from his life. He read about Rodin, about his life after banishment, about his quest to hunt down Barnabus. Everything leading up to now. All two hundred years condensed into a two-inch stack of paper.

"It's amazing," Saul said as he turned the page. "They have everything in here. It's like I'm reliving my own life. I can't believe how much we've been through."

"We have been through a lot, haven't we? Two hundred years is a long time."

Saul read another entry and laughed. "Remember the time we went apple picking, and you said you could reach the highest apple in the tree?"

"Hey, I was pretty darn close. If those squirrels had minded their own business, I would have made it, easily."

"You always blame those squirrels."

"Yeah, well you didn't do any better. You fell eight times or so, at least."

"Yeah, yeah. Don't remind me."

"And then you found that blue apple, and I convinced you it was the rarest of sweet apples."

"You have no idea how vile it tasted."

"I can't believe you believed me. You were so gullible."

"And you took full advantage."

Vince chuckled. "Of course I did. Why wouldn't I?"

Saul stared at the page, titled *Apple Picking*. "It's all in here. Everything." He sighed. "We were good friends."

"Good? We were amazing friends. Nothing less."

"That's for sure." He flipped through some more. "My life. It's had its ups, and it's certainly had its downs, but overall it's been pretty good…My life has been good. Not many people can say that. People die with regrets, wishing they had lived a different life." He looked away from the page and to the ground. "Not that I don't have regrets. I have many, but I've grown since my days in Rodin."

Vince stared at him. "You certainly have."

"And when I look back at my life, I'm happy." A single tear escaped his eye. "I know my days are numbered, but I'm happy with the life I'm leaving."

"Saul."

"It's okay, Vince. You don't have to say anything. We'll charge the Spire tomorrow and you'll go on to live the rest of your life, doing good, because you're a good person. This thing with my lung is something I can't fight. I'm going to die and I've come to accept it." More tears trickled down his face.

Vince stood up and walked over to sit next to him.

"How did Charlotte put it?" Saul continued. "We live, we play, we die. That's how it goes."

"I think she said it more eloquently than that, but you got the point. People die. That's a part of life. It's bad to kill, but it's not bad to die."

"It's bad to kill. We've killed plenty, Vince."

Vince looked down. "I know."

"So are we bad? We kill to stop others from killing, right? You killed Barnabus, and I would have done the same. That doesn't make us bad people, does it?

"No."

"So why do I feel guilty? Charlotte asked if we would stop draining once Greene is dead. I don't know if I could, but I guess I don't have a choice. I will die, plain and simple."

"Try not to think about it."

"No, that's my point. I've been trying to ignore it this whole time because I was afraid, but Charlotte is right. We shouldn't fear it. We need to make life the best it can be while it's here. And then when it's over, it's over."

Vince smiled. "You've grown so much."

They sat side by side, in their final moments before charging the Spire.

THIRTY-SEVEN

ARE ALL OF the cameras disabled?" Simon asked, looking up at the buildings.

The guard scratched his head. "All of them we could find. There are still plenty out there, but Greene has big blind spots. At least for now."

"Good enough. We just need to stay away from them while we search."

The guard continued to scratch his head. "Search for what again?"

"Christ, the sensors. Pay attention, damn it." He turned to Vince and Saul. "You two are sure this will work? They always have so many people on the walls. It's hard to find a weak spot. We've only managed to get this far with sheer numbers. Just throwing everyone we have at them."

Vince nodded. "It will work. They may appear to have lots of people, but they don't. They play artificial cheering over their speakers to create the illusion of a large army. We've seen their team. Greene has a small squad of specialized soldiers, and the rest are just volunteers. Ordinary people. These sensors activate an alarm that tells them which direction you're coming from. That's how they're always ready for you. But when you trigger more than one, it's chaos up on that wall. They're a scattered mess. If we can activate three or four at the same time, they won't know what to do. It will be the perfect time to attack."

"He will keep most of his forces at Post Five," Saul said, "where walls one and two are down. That's the weakest spot. But Post One is weak as well. That's good. It'll spread them out. With these sensors, we can hopefully thin them out even more."

"With their forces spread across the wall," Vince continued, "and using your brute numbers method, we have a good chance of overpowering them."

Simon grinned. "That bastard won't know what hit him."

"He knows we're up to something," Saul said. "It will be hard to catch him off guard, but I don't think he'll be ready for this."

Simon scanned the ground in front of him. "What exactly do these sensors look like?"

Saul shrugged. "We've never seen one. All we know is they exist."

"Then what the hell are my men supposed to look for? Your plan is useless without those sensors."

"Look for anything that looks unusual," Vince said. "It's Spire technology. It will probably have the City crest. They're laid out in an arch around the Spire, so once we find one, the rest should be easy."

"But this first one," Simon said, gritting his teeth. "How do we find this goddamn first one?"

"Just be patient."

"I have no goddamn time for patience. We need to attack Greene while he's weak."

"Believe me," Saul said. "Finding these sensors will be worth it."

"It better be."

He sent his men out across the streets to scour every corner, making sure to avoid from active cameras. Vince and Saul stayed with Simon, guiding him to possible points of interest.

"How strong are these things?" Simon asked.

"They cover the entire border around the Spire," Saul said. "So they're either strong as hell, or there are just a lot of them. It doesn't really matter for us. We just need to find one in each of the five sections."

"We don't need all five," Vince said. "Three sections should be enough. Post One and Five are already heavily defended. If we can find sensors in Two, Three, and Four, that should be enough."

"And then we attack," Simon said. "We still have bombs, but we're running low. In our previous attack, we lost a lot of supplies."

And you lost a lot of children, you crazy bastard, Saul thought to himself. "Those were impressive tactics you used against Greene."

Simon chuckled. "Greene has always been soft. That day was no different. He hesitated and paid the price. But with the third wall exposed, I can't expect to be so lucky. He may be soft, but he's not dumb. He learns from his mistakes."

"So it wouldn't work again."

"That right. And that's why your plan better work. We can't afford any screw-ups."

"It will work," Vince said with confidence. "Trust us. We want to break in just as much as you do. We want to see Greene fall. And our friends are still in there. We need to get them out."

Simon's man yelled from the other side of the block. They turned their heads to hear the distant voice.

"He must have found something," Simon said. "Come on, let's go."

They approached the man who was yelling. It was good old Crooked Tooth Jonah, holding the same turtle mug, filled with hot tea. Simon placed a hand on his shoulder. "What did you find?"

Jonah stepped aside to reveal a small mechanism, poking out of the dirt. On the top was a flashing light, and underneath, 3/2, was imprinted.

Vince knelt down to examine the device, reading the words on the side. "Invisible fence beacon," he read. "Thirty-foot-tall model." He looked up at the virtual fence that he could not see. There was a thin shadow line in the dirt, stemming from the device in both directions. It was faint, but noticeable. It ran along the center of the large street. "It must connect from beacon to beacon, like a real fence, and this is the barrier." He pointed to the line. "If we walk past this, the alarm sounds."

"Post Two on this side," Saul added, "and Post Three on this side." He pointed to the right and the left of the device.

"Ha! We already found two Posts," Simon said. "This is easier than I thought. Just one more and that sucker's as good as dead."

Vince turned to his left. "If they connect like we think they do, Post Four is this way." He bent down and pointed to the line. "But don't pass this barrier. We don't want to activate the alarm just yet. We can follow it until we reach the next beacon."

Simon looked at his men. "What are you all standing around for? You heard the man. Let's go!"

They followed the road, staying left of the shadow, and counting their paces. As they walked, Vince could tell that Simon was eager.

Saul pointed straight ahead. "There it is. It's amazing how easy they are to spot once you know what to look for."

Simon trotted ahead to examine the device. "Yes, this is what we're looking for."

Vince bent down to take a look. It was identical to the last, but it had, 4/3, imprinted instead. "Looks like we found what we need."

"If they're this easy to find," Saul said, "let's find Posts One and Five as well."

"You're right."

They both looked to Simon, who nodded. "I agree." He turned to his other men. "Find those other two beacons. I want a squad set up at each one. And don't cross that goddamn line until I give the order."

THIRTY-EIGHT

TULLY SANDERS STARED out at the buildings, listening to the empty silence. After the covert mission with Vince and Saul, it was nice to be back on the wall. He stood at Post Five, a few yards from the giant gap. A group of volunteers walked by, laughing and messing around.

"What are you doing?" Tully said. "Get back to your stations. This is serious business."

One of them looked over. "Sorry guy. We're just having some fun. We get bored standing out here all day."

"This is no time for fun. Do you understand what's at stake? Two of our walls have been breached. Simon will attack again, and if he gets through that third wall, the Spire will fall."

"Relax. There's no way he's getting through that wall."

"That's exactly the kind of thinking that got us in trouble last time. If you care about the Spire, if you care about Mr. Greene, then you will return to your stations. Otherwise, get the hell off this wall."

They slowly walked back. "Okay, calm down. We'll go back." They wandered off.

Tully leaned in towards his microphone. "Sir, these volunteers, they're not fit to defend this wall."

"I know," Greene said through his earpiece, "but we need as many people as possible. If there's one thing Simon has that we don't, it's numbers. All of those men down there have gone through basic cannon training. That should be enough, as long as they follow your lead."

The first horn sounded.

"Will they follow my lead? Those punks seemed pretty resentful when I tried to give them orders."

"You're a good soldier, Tully. And a good leader."

"I've never led untrained men before."

"Today's the day to learn. Whether you like it or not, we need those volunteers. Even with the return of you and your squad, we're still low on troops."

"Where are the rest of them?"

"I've got a squad in Snow Peak right now. Just make sure they fire those cannons and you should be fine."

"I'll do my best sir."

The horn sounded. One. Two. Three. Four. Five.

"They're coming your way," Greene said. "Get ready."

Tully turned around. "You heard the horns! Get to your stations! Now!"

They all scrambled around, obeying his direct order. Each group of three was in charge of a cannon. They began lifting the heavy cannonballs and loading them into the barrels.

"Why aren't your cannons loaded yet?" Tully yelled. "You were all sitting around when you should have been getting ready! Move it! We don't have all day!" They pushed into high gear, rolling cannonballs and tossing bricks of black powder. They ran about like confused ants trying to find their queen. "This is madness," Tully muttered to himself.

The horn sounded. One. Two.

"They're coming at Post Two," one of the men said.

"We don't have anyone stationed there," said another. "Just One and Five. We need someone over there." He waved to the others. "Come on, let's go!"

"No!" Tully yelled. "Keep your positions. Post One is closer. They can handle it." Most of the men returned, with a few stragglers sprinting off towards Post Two. "Damn it, we lost a few."

"It's okay," Greene said. "Just stay calm and focus."

Tully turned to the remaining volunteers. "The rest of you better listen to my orders, goddamn it!"

The horn sounded. One. Two. Three. Four.

They looked to Tully for orders. "This one is ours," he said and pointed to a cluster of men. "You, get over to Post Four and ready the cannons." The group ran off. Tully glanced at the ones who remained. They were running thin. "I don't have many men left, sir."

"Post One is running low as well. They're spreading us out."

"Let's just hope no more horns go off."

"If they do, make sure to—"

The horn sounded. One.

"Christ, they're coming from everywhere," Tully said.

"No, they're not. They found our sensors. They're messing with us. From now on, ignore the horns. Keep your men where they are."

The artificial cheers blared out from the speakers.

"Yes, sir." He raised his head. "Orders straight from Mr. Greene. Ignore the horns. Keep your positions." The men nodded and held their stance. "Mr. Greene, I don't think we have enough men. If they attack this post, we're screwed."

Greene did not respond.

"Someone's coming!" one of them yelled.

Tully whipped his head around. "Crap!"

Over his earpiece, he heard the two most frightening words to come from Greene's mouth. "Oh no…"

A horde of people came pouring out of the streets, towards the Spire. They screamed at the top of their lungs, holding bombs above their heads as they ran. The bare fields surrounding the Spire were quickly swarmed by Simon's men. They chanted in unison. "Crowns! Crowns! Crowns!" The rumble of stomping feet shook the ground. The noise got louder as the enemy approached.

Tully pointed to the crowd and yelled, "Fire!" The men stared at him with looks of confusion. The stomps and screams were too loud. They could not hear him. "Damn it, I said Fire!" He stepped over to the nearest cannon, pushed the man aside, and lit the wick. The blast sent the cannonball hurtling into the crowd, tearing through their bodies and spraying mists of blood. He pointed to the cannon. "Fire!"

The men finally nodded and jumped into action. A barrage of metal shot out from the wall. Cannonballs fell from the sky, crushing skulls and ripping limbs. Groups of explosions scattered among the mob sent bodies flying up in the air.

Tully watched as the men fumbled to reload the cannons. He pushed another aside, loaded the cannon himself, and fired.

"Sir," he said. "This isn't good enough. We can't hold them off. There's too many. You need to send more people to Post Five."

"I'll do what I can. I have some people already headed back your way. Not many, just a few. Post One is getting hit hard. I need troops there as well."

The mob of Crowns was approach fast. "We don't have time. They're going to get through."

"Don't let them. They mustn't get to that third wall."

"I'll do my best."

"Damn!" Greene yelled. "Post One. They've broken through the second wall."

"Already?"

"I'm moving the men back to One. They need reinforcement more than you do."

"No!" Tully begged. "I need them here. They're going to breach the wall."

"Post One is in critical condition. They need help!"

Tully stared out at the horde closing in. Explosions rose up here and there, but the mob of bloodthirsty people ran straight through. "Fire! Fire! Fire!" he yelled with intense rage. The Crowns reached the first wall and poured through the gap. He pointed down. "Aim at the bottleneck!"

They turned their cannons and fired a string of cannonballs. Spurts of blood flew up with every shot. The air was filled with specks of red mist. The metallic taste was strong on his tongue.

"We've got them at a choke point," Tully said to Greene, "but they're still getting through."

"Keep it up. You're doing better than Post One. They're hitting the third wall hard."

"Keep it up? At this rate, they'll be charging up the Spire in no time. There must be something we can do. We can't just let them in."

"I'm afraid we have no choice. Our resources are limited. We'll just have to fight them off inside and hope for the best."

"Hope for the best? That's your plan? You're supposed to have a plan for everything. What happened?"

"Vince and Saul happened. It was a mistake working with them. I should have let them die on day one when Simon had them."

"So you're giving up?

"I'm not giving up!" Greene yelled. "I'm going down with pride. I'll fight till my last breath, but I'm afraid the

Spire is done. It will fall. There's no way to avoid it. I suggest you pray. Pray that Simon will spare your life. He most certainly won't spare mine."

"I won't give him the choice, sir, because I'm going to kill him myself. You may have given up, but I haven't."

"I'm not giving up! I built the Spire from the ground up! I watched it grow from nothing to the marvel it is today! You think I want to see it fall? I will fight till my dying breath!"

Explosions hit the third wall. The ground rattled beneath Tully's feet. Smoke rose up and mixed with the smell of blood. "They've reached the third wall," someone called out, swinging his cannon around and pointing it towards the explosions.

"No!" Tully shouted as the cannonball left the barrel. It arched through the air and slammed into the wall, cracking the base. "You clod! You've damaged the thing we're trying to defend."

Another violent explosion went off. The crack grew larger, climbing up the wall. Two more blasts. It raced to the top and split apart. The stone blocks crumbled and slammed to the ground. Chunks of wall plummeted towards the Crowns below. They cheered with triumph as the boulders crushed their skulls.

Tully could not believe his eyes. Never in the history of the Spire had the third wall fallen. The Crowns climbed over bodies and debris and sprinted towards the doors of the Spire. The men on the wall abandoned their stations and ran in the direction of Post Four, looking for a safe way off the wall.

"Stand and defend!" Tully screamed. "Goddamn cowards! Stand and defend!"

They ignored him and faded into the dust. Tully was alone on the wall. *I have to get into the Spire*, he thought. *I have to protect Mr. Greene.* He ran down the nearest set of stairs and blended in with the mob that charged towards the Spire.

The crowd chanted as they ran. "Live Free Forever! Live Free Forever!" Tully kept his mouth shut and his head down, hoping no one would notice his military uniform. They reached the front doors and poured into the building. The front desk was abandoned, and the lobby was trashed with debris and garbage.

Some of the Crowns charged up the stairwell, while others waited for the elevators. Tully knew Greene was on the top floor. The elevator was the way to go. He pushed through the crowd to the elevator doors. The people around him stared up at the display. It showed the location of the lift. It rapidly counted down. 50. 40. 30. 20. 10. 1. The display beeped, and the doors slowly slid open. The crowd pushed forward, slamming Tully against the back wall of the small compartment. An unbelievable pressure pushed against his body as more people squeezed in. The doors closed and the lift shot upward.

Tully was hot and uncomfortable. The stench of sweat and blood filled the air. Pressed against the wall, he could barely breathe. Arms, legs, and elbows jutted into his side. His head was twisted back and to the right. His arm was folded behind his back. There were only sounds of coughing and panting as the people caught their breath. They looked up at the display, this time counting up. 100. 110. 120. 130. 140. 150. Another beep played before the doors opened and they all fell out.

The sudden relief of pressure on Tully's back was overshadowed by the complete terror of what he saw when he entered the hallway. Blood smeared the wall. Trails of red ran along the tile. Bodies lay scattered along the floor. Bodies of people he knew. Coworkers. Friends. The mob of Crowns ran down the corridor and turned the corner. The overhead lights flickered as he wandered down the path. From down the hall, he heard the screams of innocent people being torn apart by the angry mob.

Another beep came from behind. The second elevator. Tully stepped aside into the shadows of an empty room. He poked his head out to watch another mob stumble out of the elevator doors. He pulled his head back and waited for them to pass. They charged through, chanting the same Crown motto in unison. When they turned the corner, Tully stepped out and followed their path.

He turned the corner to another abandoned hallway with more blood and more bodies. A large steel security door was blasted in. Streaks of gunpowder lined the edges of the dented metal. Behind the security door was a set of swinging double doors. Loud cheers roared from the other side. He walked forward at a nervous pace. He did not know what he would do once he reached the doors, but he knew Greene was in danger. It was his duty to protect him.

THIRTY-NINE

VINCE AND SAUL stood by Simon as they watched the third wall fall at Post Five. Simon pointed. "They're fleeing. Now is our time."

"Do you think they've broken through at Post One?" Jonah asked.

"That doesn't matter right now. There's a clear path to the Spire and there's no one here to defend it." He jogged forward and turned around. "What are you waiting for? Let's go. We're going to kill that sucker once and for all."

Vince stepped forward. "Greene is important, but we find our friends first."

"Forget about your friends. Greene's probably killed them by now. Don't waste your time. We're making history. This is the fall of Greene. The man who's been in power for hundreds of years. This is going to be talked about for generations. We'll be known as the ones who restored justice to the City. Don't you want to be a part of that?"

Saul stood next to Vince. "Sorry, our friends come first."

Simon shook his head. "Fine. Do whatever you want. Just don't get in my way." He turned around and jogged along with the swarm of people. Vince and Saul followed and Jonah took the rear.

As they ran, a small chant began to build. "Live free forever. Live free forever." Simon joined in with them. Vince and Saul just glanced at each other and kept up with the crowd. They entered the building to see the trashed lobby. The front desk was abandoned, and the whole floor was packed with Crowns. A group was gathered around the elevators, waiting to get to the top floor.

The elevator beeped and the doors opened. They pushed their way closer until the lift was full. The doors closed and the number on the display climbed. Simon turned around. "We'll get on the next one."

"Why don't you order them out of the way?" Saul asked. "They'll let you through. You're their leader."

"I don't want to be their leader. I want Greene to fall so they can lead themselves. Once that happens, I'm just one of them. Nothing more."

"You'll be the man who brought down Greene," Vince said. "For that reason alone, people will follow you whether you want them to or not."

"That may be true, but that's their choice. It's the choice I'm fighting for them to have."

"What about the people you've killed to get here?" Saul said. "They didn't have a choice."

"Those were necessary sacrifices. You need to break a few eggs."

"Eggs? They were children. No older than ten. You killed dozens of them. Just threw them at the wall like they were nothing. They had their whole lives ahead of them, but your precious wall was more important."

"Damn right it was more important," Simon said. "Look where we are now. It worked. The Spire's in shambles, The Crowns are in control, and Greene's life is within our reach."

"Do you hear what you're saying? You may think of yourself as a hero, but you're a monster."

The people around them turned at the word *monster*.

Simon grabbed Saul's shirt and pulled him in. "Don't undermine me. Not now. Not in front of all these people."

The elevator beeped and the doors opened. They pushed forward, this time making it through the doors. The *150* button was immediately pushed. Vince pushed *149*.

Simon looked over with mild amusement. "You and your goddamn friends. I guess it's up to you."

The elevator rose as they watched the display count up. The unpleasant scent of fresh sweat filled the air. As they neared the upper floors, the people readied their weapons. Cocked their guns, drew their knives, rubbed their fists.

"Remember," Simon said to the Crowns. "No bombs inside. It's too close quarters."

The door opened to level *149*. Vince and Saul stepped out. Nobody else moved. They were all waiting for level *150*. They all wanted Greene.

Simon grinned. "Good luck. You two are on your own." He shot a grin as the door shut. The display above changed from *149* to *150* in an instant.

Vince turned around and grabbed Saul. "Come on. Let's go."

They wandered through the empty halls. No one was around. Not a single person. They passed by the testing labs, the medical sector, the briefing room, and the monitor room until they finally reached the bedroom. It was empty. Rupert, Alan, and Ella's bags sat open on their beds. Their belongings were strewn about.

Saul spun around, searching the corners of the room. "Where did they go?"

Vince shrugged. "Maybe they're hiding. Charlotte said there are safe rooms. Maybe they went there."

"They would have taken their bags, right?" Saul gestured to the scattered mess. "They wouldn't have left it like this."

"You're right. It looks like they were taken against their will."

"Of course they were taken." He said it as if it was obvious. "But where did Greene bring them? That's the question."

"To the cell room, right? That's where the labbie said they keep people. Their test subjects *and* their prisoners."

"Okay, so how do we get in there? Rupert said it's locked. We need someone with clearance."

"I assume Charlotte isn't an option after that stunt she pulled with the broadcast. She's probably down there with them."

Saul rubbed his stubble as he considered their options. "We could check the safe rooms? That's where the workers go. If Charlotte's not there, maybe someone else can help us."

"But will they? We're traitors, remember?"

Saul shrugged. "It's worth a shot. What else are we going to do?"

"Okay, let's do it." They left the bedroom and headed towards the safe room, near the testing labs. "So how do we convince them?" Vince asked.

"I don't know. Say Charlotte was lying?"

"They won't believe that. Simon announced it to the entire City, and Greene confirmed it as well. There's no way they'll believe both of them are lying."

"But they are," Saul said as they turned the corner. "We're not working for Simon. We're not working for anyone."

"But they don't know that."

"Then let's convince them. We'll tell them the truth."

"Tell them that we want to kill Simon *and* Greene? I don't think that would go over well."

"Yeah, you're right."

They arrived at the door of the safe room. "Just knock and see what happens, I guess."

Saul banged on the door. "Hey! Let us in!"

A camera was mounted just above the door. They jumped and waved in front of it, hoping someone would see them.

"We need your help!" Saul yelled. "Our friends are in danger! We need to find them, but we can't do it ourselves! We need someone who can get us into the cell room!"

After a long moment of silence, the door slid open, and a man in a white lab coat stepped out. On his chest, a name was printed. *Humphrey Jacks*. "I can help you." Others in the room peeked out from behind, confused as to why Humphrey would help these traitors. He stepped into the hallway and the door slammed shut behind him. "Follow me."

"Is Charlotte Marble in there?" Vince asked.

Humphrey shook his head. "There was a rumor going around that your friends were locked up, but no one knew for sure. They think Charlotte's down there as well. Probably because she was lying?"

"Lying about what?" Vince asked.

"About the two of you being traitors and all."

"*You* didn't believe that story?"

"Not for a second," he said as they passed the glass rooms and entered the restricted area. "You wouldn't work against Mr. Greene. You're the Heroes of the Spire. I saw you talk at the conference. You inspired all of us with your words. Especially you, Saul. There's no way two traitors could give such a genuine speech. Besides, why would you want to kill him? It just doesn't make sense. You have every reason to thank him. He gave you immortality."

Saul opened his mouth to speak, but Humphrey cut him off. "Everyone else in the safe room thought I was crazy; like I was committing treason. They don't understand that you're the good guys. But I know. And that's why I have to help you."

Vince watched Humphrey's gleeful face as they walked. "I'm glad you understand. We're not the bad guys."

"Of course not. And your friends were so nice when I met them, I knew they weren't traitors. This is all just a big misunderstanding, but I want to help make it right. If we hurry, we can stop Simon." A big goofy smile stretched across his face. "I can't believe I'm speaking face to face with Vincent Vigo and Saul Shepherd. Pinch me."

Vince and Saul exchanged looks and shrugged.

They reached the large metal door. Humphrey approached the kiosk to the side. "Okay, I just have to do a retinal scan, and then we're in." He pressed his face against the receptacle and held still for a few seconds. There was a soft buzz, and the door slid open. "Voila! And in we go."

Vince and Saul followed him in and marveled at the vastness of the room. Saul walked up to the railing and leaned over to look down. "When Rupert told us about this room, I didn't imagine anything like this. It's so big. How do we find them?"

Humphrey pointed to the sign listing the floors. "These upper levels are for test subjects. Your friends are probably being held as prisoners. Prisoners are down lower." He walked towards the stairs. "Follow me."

They did as he said, and walked down, step by step, floor by floor. They passed the testing floors and reached those with animals. Vince glanced at them behind the bars. "Is this where Fred is?"

"Rupert must have thought the same thing," Saul said.

Humphrey turned his head. "No, your friend wouldn't be here. This is strictly for animals."

Saul shook his head. "Fred is a falcon. We've been looking for her for quite a while."

"Oh yes! I remember your friend mentioned an avian companion. Fred is a very peculiar name for a female falcon."

"After we find them, let's come back here," Vince said. "We can look for her."

Saul nodded. "Sounds like a plan."

They reached the end of the animals and entered the section for prisoners. Humphrey pulled out his light to illuminate the darkness of the lower levels. "Your friends will be somewhere down here. The last I heard, these prisoner cells were pretty full. They'll be near the bottom of this section." He continued down the stairs and finally stopped. "Not down there. That's for Crown prisoners."

Vince peered down at the pitch black lower levels. "That's where *we'd* be locked up if Greene had any say."

A distant voice echoed through the empty space. "Vince? Is that you?"

Saul tilted his head to hear the voice more clearly. "It's Alan's voice. Alan! Rupert! Ella! Are you guys down here?"

"Yeah!" Alan called. "Over this way!"

They trotted towards the sound of his voice and found their cells. "I can't believe we found you," Saul said. "It's crazy out there right now."

Rupert walked to the front of his cell and grasped Vince's hand through the bars. He shook it vigorously, with a nice big smile hidden under his beard. "We didn't know if we'd ever see you again."

Ella jumped up from the ground and hopped over to greet them as well. "Last thing we heard before Greene stuck us in here, was that you two were scheduled for a public execution."

"Yes," Vince said. "But we made it through. We have Charlotte to thank for that."

"Hey," Charlotte said from the last cell over.

They walked over to her cell and leaned in. "Thank you," Saul said. "It must have been hard to defy Greene like that. To give up your retirement." He passed her journal through the bars. "This is yours."

She took it in her hands. "I couldn't have lived with myself otherwise. The way Greene set you up on that mission, it wasn't right."

"Humphrey!" Alan cheered. "My man. I knew you would come through."

Humphrey blushed. "I know you're not the bad guys. You can't be."

Alan shrugged. "I guess that's not how Greene sees it. Anyway, let's quit wasting time. Can you open these cells?"

Humphrey nodded. "Yes. I just have to go to the control room. I'll be right back." He walked off at a brisk pace.

"What's going on out there?" Ella asked. "We heard the alarms go off."

Vince leaned back against the rail of the catwalk. "It's Simon. They're in the Spire right now."

"They got through the third wall?" Alan asked. "How in the world did they do that?"

"We helped him," Saul said

"What?" all four of them said in unison.

"We told him about the sensors. About the alarm system they have set up here. We searched for them to use against Greene."

"But why?" Alan asked. "Why would you want to help Simon?"

"To rescue you guys, of course. After the way our mission went, we knew you would be in trouble. Same with Charlotte after the stunt she pulled. We're just glad he didn't kill any of you."

"Why didn't he?" Ella asked. "He has no reason to keep us alive."

"He was most likely planning an execution," Charlotte said. "He must have been waiting for something."

"At any rate," Vince said, "none of that matters right now. He hasn't killed you. We're getting you out of here."

The cell doors swung open right on cue. Alan leaped out of his cell. "I knew we could count on Humphrey!"

Rupert stepped out and looked at the floors above. "Now let's go find Fred. She's around here somewhere."

"Yes," Vince said. "We saw the animals on our way down. Had the same thought."

Humphrey came trotting back. "Sorry for the delay."

"Good work," Vince said. "Can you help us find our falcon?"

"Ah yes, your falcon. I suppose we can check those levels we passed on the way down." He walked to the stairs. "I'll lead the way."

They followed him up until they reached the floor they were looking for. Rupert ran ahead to look in each cell. "I'll check this side," he said and ran off.

The others stayed together. They didn't want to separate after just having reunited. They moved as a group and checked the cells in the other direction. There were dogs, lions, bears, and even other birds, who all looked miserable, stuffed behind bars with barely any room to move around. Each one was grimmer than the last, and they were all silent. They just stared with curiosity as the group passed by. Vince could tell from their faces, that any hope of living a free life had been beaten out of them. Life in a cage was all they knew. He could feel an energy seeping from the cells, but it was weak. A faint glow of life that could be crushed at any moment. These animals were dying.

"I really hope she's down here," Alan said. "She's been alone for so long."

Ella turned her head as they walked. "I'm getting worried about Rupert."

"If she is still in the Spire," Vince said, "this is where she'll be. Right, Humphrey?"

"Well, she wasn't in the medical sector. At least that's what your friends say. If she's not up there, she must be down here for testing."

"What kind of tests do you do on animals?" Ella asked.

"It's usually more experimental stuff. Things we're not quite ready to test on humans."

Alan shook his head. "Great, it's not safe for humans so test it on animals."

"It may sound cruel," Humphrey said, "but it works. Without these animals, we would have never advanced as far as we have. Sacrifice the wild to save those more deserving. That's Greene's philosophy and I agree."

Alan turned to Charlotte. "How do you feel about it? Do you agree?"

Her eyes shuttered. "I don't know."

"You don't know?"

"Greene has accomplished amazing things with his tests," she explained. "He's saved so many lives and made countless people happier."

"He's also angered lots of people," Alan said.

"That's true, but he means well." Her eyes sunk to the ground. "But sometimes I do question his methods." She gestured to the animals. "I question this."

"And you should," Saul said, "because it's wrong. It's just as wrong as testing on me and Vince."

"What?" Humphrey said. "But you volunteered."

He shook his head. "No, we didn't. He forced it on us. To Greene, we're just lab rats."

"Field rats," Alan corrected.

"Whatever," Saul said. "The point is, we're not rats. We shouldn't be tested on. These animals should not be tested on."

"Wait," Humphrey said. "So you didn't come to the City to thank Mr. Greene?

"No way," Saul said. "Not even close. We're here to stop him. To kill him."

Vince nudged him. "Saul don't."

He turned around, confused. "What?"

Humphrey stopped walking and looked down to his feet. "I betrayed Mr. Greene? I disobeyed orders to help the people trying to kill him?" His head rose as he realized what he had done. "I betrayed the Spire. I betrayed the City. I'm a traitor."

"You're not a traitor," Ella said. "You did what you thought was right. What *is* right. Helping us was the right thing to do, and deep down you knew it."

He backed away slowly. "No. I let my colleagues down. I let my family down. I'm a disgrace to everything Mr. Greene stands for."

"Listen   to   yourself," Saul   said.   "Greene's brainwashed you. He's not always right. You don't have to listen to everything he says. You can think for yourself."

Humphrey bumped into the rail of the catwalk and leaned his weight against it. "Simon's won. There's no place for me anymore. The Spire is my life." His hands tightly grasped around the rail. "There's nowhere left for me to go."

"Come with us," Charlotte said. "You helped us, now we can help you. These are good people. They'll protect us. We can start a new life somewhere else."

His eyes shifted to meet hers. "No." He leaned by and flipped over the rail.

"Don't!" Vince yelled leaping forward, but it was too late. Humphrey fell towards the deep abyss and was engulfed by the overwhelming darkness. Vince leaned over the rail, reaching down towards the falling body, knowing there was nothing he could do.

Saul shook his head with frustration. "Damn it! He was a good guy. Greene really messed with his head."

"A lot of people around here are like that," Charlotte said. "I used to be like that."

"It's a shame," Vince said. "These people don't deserve to be slaughtered by Simon."

"Then let's go up there and stop him," Alan said. "Both Greene and Simon."

"After we find Fred," Ella reminded them.

As the words left her mouth, a faint screech came from down the path. It was weak and distant, but it was unmistakably the screech of a falcon.

"Fred?" Ella called out. "Is that you, girl?"

Another soft screech came from a few cells down. They trotted towards the cell with excitement. As they got closer, the screeches grew faster and louder. They turned to look in the cell, and saw the bird who had separated from them on the day of the rally. The bird who had saved Vince's life from Barnabus. The bird who melted the hearts of the people in Snow Peak. It was Fred.

Alan went sprinting in the other direction. "I'll go get Rupert!" he yelled as his voice faded.

They pressed against the bars, smiling and reaching out to hold her. She hopped across the cell and jumped into Ella's arms. She embraced her, running her fingers through thick feathers, and then pulled back her hand. "Oh no."

"What is it?" Vince asked.

Ella turned Fred's body to reveal her missing wing. In its place was a small stump. "What did those monsters do to you, girl?" She held Fred up through the bars and kissed her forehead. When she placed her back down, Fred scurried up and pushed her body against the bars. "Okay girl," Ella said. "I'm not going anywhere." She picked her back up and turned to Charlotte. "Can you open this cell?"

"I should be able to, as long as they haven't taken me out of the system yet. I'll go find the control room." She tapped the bars and walked off.

Vince stared at the falcon, quivering in Ella's arms. "Why would they cut off her wing?"

Saul shook his head. "They're probably testing some regenerative crap. And clearly it didn't work. These people are sick in the head."

"It's not their fault," Ella said. "It's the only thing they've known. It sounds like Greene's been in charge for a long time. Following his orders is all they know."

"That's no excuse," Saul said angrily. "I'm sick of people following orders. I've said it before, and I'll say it again, these people need to think for themselves. Come up with their own thoughts. Make their own decisions. Greene's not a god. He's just a man."

"He may be just a man," Vince said, "but he's still powerful."

"*Was* powerful," Saul corrected. "With the Crowns in the Spire, it looks like he's about to lose his power."

"And the power will fall into Simon's hands," Ella said. "Not much better. I'd say it's even worse."

Vince shook his head. "Simon says he doesn't want power. He just wants Greene to lose his. He wants to give the people the choice to do what they want."

"Right," Saul said. "That's exactly what they need, but I don't think he'll follow through. He's had control of the Crowns for too long. He's used to having power. I don't think he'll give it all up that easily."

Ella looked back down to Fred. "I don't see how any of this can end well. If Simon kills Greene, or if Greene kills Simon. If Simon keeps his power, or if he decides to give it away. Whatever happens, the City can't survive, right?"

"If they both die," Vince said. "That's the only way. Then the City has a chance."

Saul nodded. "Then we'll just have to make sure that happens. Once Fred is out of this cell, we go up there and kill whoever is left. Then we get the hell out of here."

The cell door clicked and Ella swung it open. Fred fluttered her wing and wobbled out of the cell, into Ella's arms. As Ella caught her, they heard rapid footsteps. They turned to see Rupert, running in their direction, Alan trotting behind him. Fred jumped to the ground and ran with excitement. Rupert stumbled to the ground and wrapped his arms around her, kissing her beak. Fred let out a screech of joy as he showered her with love.

Rupert turned her body to get a closer look at her wing. "What happened? Her wing is gone." He stared at them, but they gave no answer. "They cut off her wing?" His face turned red. "Why would they do that?"

They gathered around, channeling feelings of joy and anger. Joy that Fred was no longer alone. Anger that Greene had tormented her. Their next move, go up and make him pay.

FORTY

TULLY GLARED AT the double doors at the end of the hallway. Behind him, another distant beep rang from the elevator, followed by another loud mob. Again, he stepped into the shadows and waited. The crowd got louder as they passed by. Tully peeked out, and what he saw shocked him. Simon. It was the first time he had seen Simon up close. He was more intimidating in person than he was on television. He was bigger. More intense.

He watched them push through the double doors and disappear into the next room. He looked up and saw the sign hanging above the doors. *Victor Greene*. It was Greene's office. He was probably in there at that very moment, with a mob full of angry Crowns, and they all wanted to kill him. Tully jumped forward and sprinted at the door, slamming through and bursting into the middle of the room.

Everyone stared at him in silence. He looked around, searching for Greene. He saw Crowns. He saw Simon. He saw bombs and guns. He saw dozens of troops in his squad lying dead in pools of blood. And then he saw Greene, lying on the floor, arms and legs bound. His face was bruised and swollen, and blood trickled from his nose.

"Who the hell are you?" Jonah said.

Simon looked up and down at his uniform. "He's a soldier. One of Greene's. Tie him up."

Three men grabbed Tully from behind, and one kneed him in the gut. He fell to the ground like a ton of bricks, holding his stomach. Spit drooled from his mouth as he moaned with pain.

Simon watched him squirm on the ground and laughed. "Pathetic. You've never been hit in the stomach before? You're a goddamn soldier!" He turned to Greene. "This is why you've failed. You're weak, and it's rubbed off on your soldiers. Everyone in the Spire is a coward because of you." He shrugged and stepped closer. "But I guess that's what happens. The strong survive, and the weak shrivel up and die."

He kicked Greene in the stomach and turned back to Tully. His men had just finished tying and gagging him. "You're weak, but you're loyal. I'll give you that. You knew we'd be up here, and you knew there were a lot of us, but you came anyway. By yourself too. You really must love this man. Either that or you're just stupid. It doesn't really matter, I suppose. Either way, you're on the wrong side." He approached Tully as he spoke. "Tell me, what's your name? Wait, no, I change my mind. Don't tell me. I don't want to know. They say not to name animals that you know are going to die. It makes it harder when they do. Of course, my men would still kill you, I just wouldn't be able to watch." He beat on his chest. "My little old heart couldn't take it." He shook his head. "So no names, because I want to watch. It's too much fun to miss. Don't believe me? Here, let me show you."

He drew his gun, pointed it at Greene's head, and pulled the trigger. A burst of light flashed from the barrel and a loud pop filled the room. Greene's head exploded in chunks of brain and skull. Blood spilled from his bottom half and stained the carpet in deep red.

Tully cried out in horror, muffled by his gag. He watched his leader, his boss, his friend, lie headless on the ground in front of him. The body still twitched. The arms and legs jerked up and down. Tears poured down Tully's face. His chest ached, and he wanted to vomit.

Simon watched Tully's reaction. "See? I told you it was fun. Getting a little worked up there, are you? Squeamish? No, I'm sure you've seen plenty of dead bodies. I guess you really did just love him." He shrugged. "Sorry I called you stupid. I didn't let Greene have any last words, but you seem like a smart guy. I think I'll give you the privilege." He pulled off Tully's gag.

Tully shivered. "You're a monster."

"Don't waste your last words on something so juvenile. I know, I'm a monster. Everyone's been saying that lately." He looked deep into Tully's eyes. "I'll give you one more shot. Last words? And make them count because I'm losing my patience."

Tully glared back with a burning hatred. "You think you're—"

Simon raised his gun. "Nope, changed my mind." He pulled the trigger.

FORTY-ONE

VINCE. SAUL. CHARLOTTE. Rupert. Ella. Alan. Fred. They all stood in the elevator, waiting for the count on the display to reach *150*. Whatever awaited them would change things forever. By the end of the day, someone would die. Greene? Simon? Maybe both. Either way, they would find out soon.

Saul gripped one of the many guns on his body. "Good idea stopping off at the supply room."

Vince examined his own gun. He carried only one modest handgun. "I wasn't sure if we'd access without Humphrey, but it looks like Charlotte's still in the system."

"Another half day and they'd probably wipe me from the records," She said.

Alan awkwardly held his gun. It was larger than he was comfortable with. "Let's just hope that luck sticks around."

"Do we have a plan?" Ella asked. "We can't just go in firing. That'll surely get us killed."

"We don't know who's on top right now," Vince said. "If it's Greene, our plan is simple. There's no negotiating with him. We pop in, shoot him, and get out as quickly as possible. But if Simon's in charge, things are a little trickier. Saul and I have somewhat of a deal with him. We can request a private meeting, with just him and us. No troops. Once we're alone, we take him out."

Rupert looked down at Fred, who was nestled deep in his arms. He was the only one without weapons. "That sounds like a plan."

"Rupert and Charlotte will stay back," Vince continued. "Obviously, Rupert needs to look after Fred."

"Why do I stay back?" Charlotte asked.

"Because of that broadcast you made. To Simon's troops, you're the one who blew our cover. You sabotaged our *mission* with Simon. If Simon is in control up there, if any of the Crowns recognize you, our plan is compromised. We need someone to watch the halls anyway, to make sure no one sneaks up on us."

"I'm the only one who's used a gun before," she said. "You need me in that room."

"I've used one before. I killed Barnabus."

"But you seemed pretty shaken up by it. Both of you struggled with the bloodshed we saw on the wall. What makes you think this will be any different?"

"We're trying to avoid bloodshed whenever possible. In order to do that, you can't be in that room with us. Don't worry. We'll call if we need help."

The elevator beeped and the doors opened to an empty hallway. Dead bodies were scattered along the sides, and blood smeared the walls and ceiling. The lights flickered, and the air was filled with dust and debris. They stepped out and walked down the corridor, staring at the carnage as they passed by. The silence was uncomfortable, but they were all afraid to break it.

They reached the end and turned the corner, where they saw the remnants of a large security door, similar to the one for the cell room. It was completely blasted in. Black streaks of powder lined the edges. Behind the security door was a set of double doors. From the ceiling hung a sign. *Victor Greene.* Vince pointed, and they all nodded.

The choice was clear. They could turn back now. Return to the elevator and get the hell out. But they had come too far to run now. They owed it to themselves, to the City, and to Patrick. So they did not turn back. Instead, they moved forward, towards a room full of people who wanted them dead.

Vince pressed his hand against the door. He signaled for Rupert and Charlotte to stay back. They nodded and positioned themselves on either side of the door. Vince waved at the others and pushed through the door.

They entered a room full of Crowns. On one side was the dead body of a familiar face. Tully Sander. There was a hole right through his temple. On the other side, Simon stood over another body. Greene. The top half of his skull was completely blown off. The Crowns raised their guns and pointed them at Vince as he entered.

Simon threw his arms in the air. "Vince! Saul! You made it!" He gestured to his men. "Lower your weapons. They're not our enemies." They obeyed and stepped back, one of them accidentally bumping a button on the wall. A voice called out.

Evacuation Pod A. Please verify your identity.

Simon ignored it. "I see you found your friends." His eyes lowered to the weapons in their hands. "And you've picked up a few other things as well."

"Just to be safe," Vince said. "Greene's men are all over the place."

"Not up here, as you can see." He gestured to the abundance of Crowns. "You missed all of the fun. I know your friends are important, but man, when I sent that bullet through Greene's head, that is something you can only truly experience in person."

"So what now?" Saul asked.

"What now?" he repeated. "Now we clean out the Spire. Wipe out the straggling workers and free the prisoners. That's why we're here in the first place, right?"

"I mean between us. Where do we go from here?"

"Oh," Simon said. "I haven't put much thought into that."

Vince looked around at all of the Crowns watching them. "Can we discuss it with fewer people around?"

Simon furrowed his brow and stared at Vince. "You mean speak in private?"

"Yes, if you don't mind."

His eyes dropped back down to the gun his hand. "Why?"

Vince shrugged. "I just think it's a private matter."

Simon squinted. "Two of them stay. The rest leave."

"Fair enough."

Simon waved at his men to leave, and they emptied out in an orderly fashion. Rupert and Charlotte stepped behind the doors as they swung open, and remained hidden as Crowns marched out.

Once they were alone, Simon turned to Vince. "What are you morons up to? You came up here, head to toe with firepower. Why? You saw how many men there were in the elevator. There was no doubt we would overpower Greene. So that means you came armed to the teeth, for me."

Vince stepped forward. "I can—"

Simon raised his gun, and his men did the same. "Don't come any closer!" Vince and the others raised their hands over their heads. "You think I'm stupid? You tried to poison me back at headquarters. You're probably trying to poison me right now, or something like that."

Vince patted his pocket and felt the extra capsule inside.

"And these guns are just your backup plan. Well, I hate to break it to you, but both plans failed. Drop all of your weapons." He waved his gun at them. "Slowly. Lay them on the ground. All of them."

They listened to his orders and carefully placed their weapons on the ground.

"Good," Simon said, lowering his gun. He gathered the pile and tossed them across the room. "This is quite unfortunate for all of you. I was going to let you free. I kill Greene, you rescue your friends, and we go our separate ways. That was the deal. But this dumb little stunt changes everything. If I let you go now, you'll just come back later."

Saul stepped forward. "We're not here to kill you."

"Please. From the minute I met you I knew you didn't like me. Especially this one." He pointed to Ella.

"That may be true," Saul said, "but people change. We realized that Greene was the one who needed to die, not you. Your vision for the City is what everyone needs. The freedom to choose. Live free forever."

Simon's suspicious glare lingered a bit longer, and popped back to a jovial laugh. "I'm glad," he said as he slowly paced around the room. "I was worried we'd butt heads once Greene was out of the picture, but I can see that's not the case. Am I right Ella?"

Ella nodded. "Yes, sir. All we want to do is go home, and let the City live the life you've offered them."

"Exactly," he said, still strolling about. "That's all I want. Choice. Freedom. For everyone. If anyone gets in the way of achieving that, we have a problem."

"Of course," Saul said. "And we have no intention of getting in your way. Like she said. We just want to go home."

Simon now walked along the edge of the room, sliding the tip of his gun against the wall. "Yes, home. That's the place to be. Of course, Rodin is very far."

"I suppose Rodin isn't home for us anymore," Saul said.

"Then where is home?"

"I don't know. We've been traveling for so long. Moving from town to town. I guess we've spent the longest time here, in the City, but I wouldn't call it home."

Simon shook his head. "No, this isn't your home. You're outsiders. You don't have a home. At least, not anymore. It really is a shame." He wandered up behind Saul. "You say you want to go home, but you have nowhere to go." He pointed his gun at Saul's head and pulled the trigger.

Saul's skull exploded in a mist of blood.

The gunshot rang in Vince's ears as he watched the body fall to the ground. His froze, unable to move a single muscle. His friend for over two hundred years was dead. Gone in an instant.

"I can see right through your lies," Simon said, wiping the blood off his face. As he moved the gun towards Vince, Charlotte and Rupert came bursting through the door.

Charlotte shot at Simon from across the room. Simon turned and ducked for cover. His two men raised their guns. Charlotte moved her aim and pierced one of them through the chest. The other managed a single shot before Ella charged in and knocked him to the ground. The bullet whizzed by Charlotte's head. Ella grabbed the gun from his hands and jammed the end into his face.

Alan ran up and kicked Simon in the stomach, forcing him to his knees. Swarms of men charged in through the entrance, all fully armed. "Come on!" Alan yelled. "We need to get out of here!"

Charlotte and Rupert ran to the end of the room and pressed the button on the wall. *Evacuation Pod A. Please verify your identity.* Charlotte held her eyes against the scanner and waited for the door to open. A panel in the wall slid up, revealing a small compartment with a seat and flashing buttons. They got inside. "Let's go!" she yelled.

Alan grabbed Vince's arm, who was still trapped in a state of shock. His face was blank, his eyes lifeless. Alan pulled, but he would not budge. Ella ran over and grabbed his other arm, throwing it over her shoulder. "We'll carry him," she said. Alan nodded and did the same. They dragged him to the pod and placed him in the seat.

The horde of Crowns flooded the room. Jonah bent down to check on Simon, who shook him off. "I'm fine you idiot. Get *them*!"

They looked up to the pod and raised their guns. Charlotte slammed her fist against a button. A glass door slid down just as they opened fire. The bullets hit the glass and bounced off. "Don't worry," Charlotte said. "It's bulletproof." She pressed another button.

Evacuation Pod A will eject in thirty seconds.

"Thirty seconds?" Alan said. "Why does it take so long? Let's go now!"

"It has to detach from the building," She said. "Don't worry. We're completely safe in here. Guns can't hurt us while we're behind this glass."

Simon stood up and held up his hand. "Hold your fire."

Evacuation Pod A will eject in twenty seconds.

Simon walked over to Jonah and spoke into his ear.

"What is he doing?" Ella asked.

Jonah smiled, reached into his back pocket, pulled out a bomb, and handed it to Simon.

"Crap," Alan said. "I don't suppose this glass is bombproof as well."

Charlotte stared at Simon. "I don't know."

He lit the fuse, wandered over to the pod, and propped it up against the glass. He backed away and crossed his arms. A smirk crept across his face.

Evacuation Pod A will eject in ten seconds.

Rupert glared at the fuse as it burned down. "Are we going to make it?"

Charlotte gripped the side of the control panel. "I don't know, but you better hold on to some—"

The ground shook violently, and a loud blast filled their ears. The outside of the glass was shrouded in smoke and fire. A crack formed at the base, but it remained intact. When the smoke cleared they could see Simon. He saw the crack and slammed his foot down. "Goddamn it!" he yelled.

Evacuation Pod A ejecting.

The pod shifted outward and shot away from the building. They flew away from the Spire with incredible speed, out towards the water. A parachute opened and jerked the pod upward. As they floated down, they gazed at the exterior of the Spire. At the crumbling remains of the surrounding three walls. At the army of Crowns pouring into the lobby. Greene's reign was over.

The pod gently plopped down, and the floor quickly filled with water.

"There's a leak," Charlotte said. "That bomb must have blown a hole in the floor."

"Will we be okay?" Alan asked.

She shook her head. "These things are designed to float, but this damage is critical. The water is filling fast. We need to find something else."

"Look," Ella said. She pointed to the gap in the outer wall. The same gap they had entered through when they first found the City.

"We're not going back in that way," Alan said. "The Crowns will tear us apart."

"No," Ella insisted. "Look. Our raft is still there."

The wooden raft, crafted from remnants of the boat, sat right where they left it, sitting atop a pile of debris.

"Fantastic," Rupert said, looking down at his feet. "Let's grab it before we're waist deep in water."

Charlotte tinkered with the controls. "This thing should have water control. If I find it, we can drive over."

"You better hurry up," Alan said. "It's filling up fast."

"Just give me a minute. I've never used this model before. We haven't had a drill since we last upgraded."

"Here's a suggestion for the next upgrade," Alan said, "Make that stupid countdown shorter."

"We made it out in one piece. That's what matters." She looked to Vince, who was stiff as a board. He stared straight ahead, not a single word spoken. "But not all of us made it out," she said, placing a hand on his shoulder. "I've watched Saul for a good portion of his life. He was a good man."

"He sure was," Alan said. "I think that's something we can all agree on."

The pod engine hummed and pushed them forward.

"Got it!" Charlotte said.

They moved closer to the wall. Closer to the smoke and explosions. Closer to the screams and hollers. Closer to the chaos they just escaped.

When they reached the wall, the water was up to their knees. They stepped out of the pod one by one. Vince remained in his seat. Ella walked over and patted his back. "Come on Vince. Time to get up." He blinked a few times and got up on his own. He stepped onto solid ground with the others, but remained silent.

Last in the pod was Charlotte. She hoisted herself up, ready to join the others on land, when she heard a shuffle in the corner, under the control panel. She peeked under. "Oh my god."

"What is it?" Ella asked, leaning over to see.

Charlotte moved to the side and a young girl stepped out of hiding. She was short and skinny, with gold hair and blue eyes. Freckles covered her puffy face. Charlotte took her shoulder and leaned in closely. "How old are you, honey?"

Her body shivered, dripping from head to toe. "I don't know."

"She looks about seven years old," Rupert said. "Maybe a little older."

"What's your name?" Charlotte asked

"Izzy," she answered. Her voice was soft and delicate. "Izzy Greene."

They all stopped and looked up.

"Greene?" Charlotte asked. "Are you related to Victor Greene?"

She nodded. "He's my dad. He told me to wait in the pod. He said he would be right back. But he never came."

Charlotte looked at her face, heartbroken. "Okay. Let's get you out of this water." She lifted her up and handed her to Ella. Once Charlotte was out, she joined the group and shrugged. "I didn't know he had a daughter. No one knew."

Ella bent down to meet Izzy's eyes. "Where have you been living?"

"With dad, in the Spire. He said it was dangerous to leave."

"You've lived up there for ten years?"

A rumbling explosion went off close by. The ground shook and dust puffed up in the air. Alan tapped Ella's shoulder. "We can ask questions later. Right now we need to get the hell out of here."

The evacuation pod sunk below the waves, as they pushed their old raft back into the water. They boarded the raft and pushed away from the wall. Alan waved his hand at the City. "See you never."

Charlotte glanced at him, "We're going back, you know. We have to. Once things settle down."

Alan turned to the others. "No, we're not going back. Right? That place is a mess."

"That mess is my home. I've never left those walls before. The City is all I know. And now it's in the hands of a madman."

"He doesn't want the power," Rupert said. "He's not going to rule."

"That's what he says," Charlotte said, "but will he follow through? I doubt it. And if he does, that might be worse. The City can't survive without a leader."

"We know the City is your home," Ella said, "but it's not ours. We have a home back in Snow Peak. We have friends and families waiting for us."

Charlotte lowered her head. "I understand. I'll follow you back to Snow Peak, and stay for a day or two, and then I'll return on my own."

"If you change your mind, you're always welcome to live with us. You're one of us now."

"Thank you. You are all great friends."

Alan looked at Izzy, who was huddled up in the corner of the raft. "What are we going to do with her?"

"Bring her back with us," Rupert said. "What other option do we have? We can take care of her in Snow Peak."

Izzy's eyes widened. "I want to go home. I want to see my dad."

They all looked down. None of them had the heart to tell her. Charlotte held her arms. "Honey, your father has moved on."

"What do you mean, moved on?"

"He's passed away."

Her eyes began to water. "What?" She tried to speak, but the words were only mumbles as tears poured from her eyes. Charlotte leaned in to hug her, rocking back and forth against the waves of the ocean. The others watched, all too sad to say anything

As they sailed through the water in a bout of sorrow, Vince watched the City in the distance. He watched the endless wall. The Spire. The smoke. The explosions. It was the same scene he had watched coming in, only this time, Saul was not by his side.

To Be Concluded in…

Pick up *Vigo's Lament* today to learn more about Greene's mysterious daughter. For more information, visit:

www.tothemoonpublish.com/vigos-lament

Want More?

For news on upcoming books, sign up for Moon Mail at:

www.tothemoonpublish.com/moon-mail

Did you leave a review?

Written reviews greatly help a book get noticed. If you enjoyed this book and would like to help me out, please leave a review and let others know about the series. Thank you for supporting me!

About The Author:

 Chris Yee grew up in Needham, Massachusetts. As a young child, he had a wild imagination, thinking up stories of mystery and wonder. People would ask what he wanted to be when he grew up, and the answer was always the same. He wanted to be an author.

As he grew older, educational interests pulled him away from the world of writing and into math and science. He attended Northeastern University and received a Bachelor's Degree in civil engineering. He now works in Boston, full-time as an engineer. Despite his technical background, he never lost an interest in writing. He writes every day, to fulfill a passion that has never faded.